THE SPIRIT
IS WILLING

Also by Max McCoy

Of Grave Concern

THE SPIRIT
IS WILLING

MAX MCCOY

KENSINGTON PUBLISHING CORP.
http://www.kensingtonbooks.com

Dodge is the Deadwood of Kansas; her incorporate limits are the rendezvous of all the unemployed scalawagism in seven states; her principal business is polygamy without the sanction of religion; her code of morals is the honor of thieves, and decency she knows not . . . The employment of many citizens is gambling, her virtue is prostitution and her beverage is whiskey.

—Frank C. Montgomery, Editor,
Hays (Kansas) City Sentinel

None but the dead are permitted to tell the truth.

—Mark Twain

PROLOGUE

In my dreams, I see the book.

I'm at the bottom of a ditch in a haze-shrouded wood and the sun is a guttering flame beyond the trees. My feet are sunk up to my ankles in mud and every step is punctuated by a sucking, slapping sound. There is a strange smell, like warm copper and rotten eggs. I am not alarmed, at least not at first, just confused. How did I get here?

Unsure of which direction to turn, I call out, but there is no answer, just my voice echoing in the trees. Taking another step, my foot catches in the mire and I fall to my hands and knees, fouling my white dress in the muck. Then my hands find something in the shadows in the bottom of the trench, a familiar rectangular shape, and I bring it up. It's a book, a big one, bound in red Moroccan leather and with the title in gilt lettering. I marvel that such a treasure has been left so carelessly in such a forsaken place, and I brush my fingertips over the red leather and the golden letters.

But I can't read the title.

Oh, I can identify some individual letters—an S *here, an* X, *and a* W—*but I just can't make sense of them. I shake my head in disbelief. I don't know what's wrong with me. I open the book and scan first one page and then another, but it's all the same, except for the page numbers, which end at 307. But the text might as well be written in ancient Greek, for all the sense I can make of it. Frustration washes over me like a river. I know I must solve the riddle, but how can I, stuck at the bottom of this ditch in an unfamiliar wood?*

Then I begin to notice that there are other objects around me, sharp objects that stab my feet and ankles when I try to walk. I nudge one of these with my bare foot in the mud and realize that is made of bone and teeth. I look down and see the bottom of the trench is littered with human bones—femurs, shoulder blades, broken skulls . . . jawbones.

There are other sharp things in the trench. A mass of rifles and bayonets. Revolvers and swords. Clusters of grapeshot, lengths of chain, and iron fragments of exploded shells.

Then it begins to rain. The drops splatter on the open pages of the book in my hands, each leaving a bright red stain. I close the book and cross my arms over it, trying to shield it. But it's no use—the blood is everywhere, running down my face like sin and staining my dress crimson. Only now I realize the dress is really a wedding dress.

That's when I woke.

I had the dream the night before the Sky Pilot

came. I sat up in bed, terrified and trembling. I reached for the pencil and ledger I keep by my bed in the rented room at the Dodge House and scrawled, in the darkness in a sleep-drunk hand, the words that were still ringing in my mind.

I see rain the color of red, red blood.

1

On the first day of summer, when the frying pan of Kansas was just beginning to sizzle, and the people of Dodge City were keeping to the shadows, and the saloons and gambling halls and brothels of Front Street had yet to roar, a sun-beaten man cradling a sweat-stained King James Bible stumbled and fell hard on the wagon ruts in front of the China Doll bordello.

"Sweet Jesus," he cried.

The bawds came spilling from the front door like a magician pulling silk scarves from a hat, a flurry of color in an otherwise drowsy street cast in shades of dust. The girls puddled around the stricken man like butterflies. He protested weakly and extended a scabby finger toward the book, which had bounced from his hand and now lay tented just beyond his reach.

"Give me," he croaked.

The girls laughed and rolled him over onto his back.

The man's beard was matted, his dark hair was thick and greasy, and his lips were cracked and bloody. His dark clothes were of good quality, but stiff with dirt and streaked by sweat stains, and there was a ragged hole in the fabric over his left knee.

An auburn-haired girl cradled his head in her lap, while the others made soft nonsense sounds and gently placed their hands upon him. There were two blondes, a brown-haired girl, and a green-eyed celestial. The man's mad dark eyes studied their faces, each in turn, the three white girls and the mulatto and the lone celestial, and he was wondering perhaps why he was chosen for this bit of comfort, or whether he was about to be carried to his last reward in the arms of angels. But it wasn't their hearts that were made of gold; these girls were entrepreneurs, and while they spoke soothingly to him, they were running their hands through his pockets, searching for legal tender.

"C'est le bordel," I muttered in French. It was an appropriate phrase because it literally refers to brothels, but means "What a mess."

I had been sitting in the cane chair on the porch in front of my agency window when I saw the man fall. I had been reading a story about an eclipse in a week-old paper from Kansas City, but I had a hard time following it because I hadn't slept well the night before. I had draped a wet kerchief around my neck in an attempt to keep cool, my favorite green one with the Paisley print, but it had little effect against the oppressive heat. For these reasons and more (the more would be a man named Calder) I was in a bad temper, but I couldn't leave the unfortunate man to the furies who had descended upon him. I was acquainted with the girl with the red hair because of a case from the previous winter, and although we shared the same color of tresses, the similarities ended there. The others I knew by reputation, if not by name. Throwing down the paper, I crossed the street and addressed the denizens of the China Doll.

"Hands off, girls," I said.

"Just because him a Sky Pilot don't mean that he beyond the quarantine line," said the girl I recognized. She called herself Hickory Lane and her voice was thick with the hills and hollers of Arkansas, and when she drank—which was only when she was awake—her sentences became laden with an extra helping of indefinite articles. "We all a had plenty of them preachers in the China Doll before and they not a one of them let that black book get between nature's intent and them a Sunday school lessons."

Hickory stood, letting the man's head drop onto the hard road with a sound like a ripe melon. She took a step or two back, but still held her defiant chin in the air.

"You were picking the pockets of a man who is half burned up and defenseless," I said.

"Still a man, ain't him?" Hickory shot back. "You a think he would shy from taking vantage of any one of us if'n he found us on our backs and outa our heads sick? Reckon him a get what is deserved."

"Don't matter anyway," the brown-haired girl said. "He didn't have nothin'."

"Fetch some water."

"Gets it your own a self," Hickory said.

"No time for your foolishness, Hickory," I said. "Fetch some water, please."

Hickory folded her freckled arms and shifted her weight to one ample hip. The other girls had drawn back and seemed less confident. They exchanged glances and small words among themselves. The oriental girl, who the others called Rose, nodded and ran inside the house.

Hickory shook her head.

"Think a you're something, don't you?" she asked me. "You got a you another little mystery here, don't you? Where this Sky Pilot have a come from, what is a his name, and what him a doin' burning on the prairie? But all a your parlays with haints and your fancy man a clothes make you no different than a rest. You just another cat with a bad case of curious."

"For goodness' sake, Hickory," I said, although I may have used language a bit stronger than that, "hold your fire until later. There's a sick man here."

Hickory cleared her throat and spat theatrically in the dust.

"All this compassion has a left me dry," she

said, and ambled off in the direction of the Saratoga saloon.

Kneeling next to the Sky Pilot, I took the green kerchief from my neck and draped the dampish cloth over his balding head. His skull gimbaled back on his neck to look into my eyes, and his lips formed a word.

"Help."

"Water's coming," I said.

He shook his head.

"Book."

I motioned for the Bible, and one of the blondes—her name was either April or May, I could never remember—picked it up from the dusty street and handed it to me. I placed the book on the Sky Pilot's chest, and he folded his hands over it.

"Thank you," he said.

Black-haired Rose came flying out of the house with an earthenware pitcher and a tin cup. I filled the cup and held it up to the man's battered lips, allowing him just a sip.

"Not too fast," I said.

He drank a bit, then coughed, then drank some more.

"Somebody get Doc McCarty," I called over my shoulder.

April—or was it June?—volunteered and set off down the street.

I looked down at the Sky Pilot and smiled, despite the stench from his skin and clothes. It was difficult to guess his age, because his face had been creased and broken by the sun, but his eyes—which were wide and dark and warm as walnuts—had a curious childlike quality.

"What happened to you?" I asked.

"The sun," he said.

"I know," I said. "How long were you alone on the prairie?"

"Wasn't alone," he said. "God was with me."

"And He couldn't lead you to water?"

"I thirsted," he said, then had to pause because his voice cracked. He took another sip of water. "I thirsted for righteousness, and was filled."

He stared up at me with a disturbingly beatific smile.

Rose came with McCarty in tow, her silk robe flapping immodestly about her thighs. Doc had one hand clamping his hat on top of his head and the other clutching his Gladstone bag.

"Slow down, Rose," McCarty pleaded.

Doc knelt on one knee and placed his hand on the man's forehead, then used a thumb to draw back an eyelid.

"What's your name?"

The Sky Pilot blinked in confusion.

"When's the last time you made water?"

"Don't know," he said.

Rose tried to give him more water, but Doc stopped her.

"Did he tell you anything, Ophie?" Doc asked me.

"Not much. Said he was out talking with God on the prairie."

"Delirium," Doc said.

He put his hands against the man's throat to feel his pulse.

"Rapid."

Doc removed his stethoscope from the Gladstone, hooked the tubes in his ears, and let the instrument dangle while he undid the buttons of the man's shirt, from the belt buckle up. When he came to the Bible, he took the book from man's grasp and handed it to me.

"Hold this, please," Doc said.

The covers of the Bible were stiff as boards. Perhaps it was the amount of sweat and dirt the cover had absorbed, or perhaps it had gotten wet.

Doc slipped the business end of the stethoscope beneath the fabric of the man's shirt. "Will he live?" Rose asked.

Doc shushed her with the forefinger of his free hand.

Long seconds passed as he listened with intent. I liked the way Doc worked; he was businesslike and efficient, but was never in a hurry. He made it seem like the only patient he ever had was the one who was in front of him at the time. Then I wished that someone would pay that kind of attention to me, and the thought filled me with guilt, because I was jealous of the wretched man on the ground.

Doc removed the tubes from his ears, folded the stethoscope, and tucked the instrument back into the Gladstone.

"You'll recover," he told the Sky Pilot. "But it

will take time, and it's not going to be pleasant. Not only are you suffering from a terrible sunburn, you're also dehydrated. You're going to have to suck on ice chips for a spell before you can drink water, or it'll make you sicker. We can bathe you in tea and chamomile to ease the burn, but we'll have to watch for skin infections. Do you have somebody to take care of you?"

The Sky Pilot blinked.

"Do you understand any of what I've told you?" Doc asked louder. "You're going to need a place to stay, and medicine, and somebody to care for you."

"God will look after me."

"Is there no one made of flesh and blood to care for you?"

He shook his head.

"Where's your family?" Doc asked. "From whence did you come?"

"I don't know," the Sky Pilot said. "Can't remember."

"Anything in his pockets?"

"Girls already went through them," I said. "They found nothing."

"Maybe there's an answer in that book of his."

"There is," the Sky Pilot said. "For you, and every other living soul."

The Bible was about the size of a cigar box, too small to be a family Bible, but about the right size for a presentation Bible, and there probably was an inscription. I opened the front cover, but discovered the first few pages had been ripped out, including the entire books of Genesis and Exodus.

"What happened to the first couple of dozen pages?" I asked.

"Not by bread alone," the Sky Pilot said.

"Meaning what?" Doc asked.

"But by every word of God."

"Talk sense," Doc ordered.

"I devoured them."

"You ate them," Doc said.

"I did," the Sky Pilot said, beaming.

Doc sighed.

"A bibliophage. That's a first for me."

"Will it hurt him?" Rose asked.

"I don't think there's anything in paper or ink that would do permanent damage, but I can think of easier ways to digest one's religion."

"Do you know Jesus, Doctor?"

"I won't discount any remedy in a medical crisis."

"How about you, sister?" the Sky Pilot asked, turning his attention to me. He reached and grasped the front of my shirt with surprising force and pulled me toward him. His breath was as dry and hard as the Old Testament. "Have you been saved?"

"Like Paul," I said, "I am working on my own salvation with fear and trembling."

I tried to pull away, but his grip was fast.

"Pray hard, sister. Time is short!"

"Mind the shirt," I said. "Prayer won't pay the laundry to mend it."

"Come with me," he said, trying to rise. "To the river! The Arkansas is our River Jordan, and I shall baptize thee and the heavens will open and a voice will be heard!"

"Son, she ain't Him," Doc said. "Now, settle down before we have to knock you down."

He released his grip and his hand fell to the ground as if it were a bird that had been taken in flight.

"Preacher, I don't think you appreciate the danger you're in," Doc said. "Pay some heed to what I'm saying."

"I understand what you've said," the Sky Pilot replied. "But Jesus said to take no thought for your own life. Would you read it for me, sister?"

"Pardon?"

"Read it," he said.

"You haven't eaten it yet?" I asked.

"Are you familiar with the passage?"

"Luke, Chapter 12."

"You know your Bible."

I didn't tell him it was a necessity in my past profession as a con woman. Being able to quote the Bible with authority inspired trust, and came in handy when someone challenged your motives.

"It would be a comfort to hear the words," he urged.

I hesitated.

"Please," Rose urged. "He wants it."

"Oh, all right," I said. "But he has to promise to stop this foolishness."

I opened the stiff book and thumbed the yellowing and dog-eared pages to the New Testament. In a moment, I had found the chapter and verse.

"'Take no thought for your life,'" I read. "'Consider the ravens: for they neither sow nor reap; which neither have storehouse nor barn; and God feedeth them: how much more are ye better than the fowls?'"

"Amen," the Sky Pilot said.

"You're going to Amen yourself into feeding the turkey buzzards if you don't start tending your health," Doc said. "That would be akin to taking your own life, and you know what your book says about that."

"Ecclesiastes," the Sky Pilot nodded. "Don't be overly wicked, and don't be foolish. Why should one die before one's time?"

"He is howling mad," Doc said. "And I'm all out of notions."

"What will happen to him?" Rose asked.

"He can't care for himself, and he hasn't the money to pay someone to look after him," Doc said. "I reckon the city marshal will have to lock him up in the city jail until somebody can figure out what to do with him."

Silence fell like a wet burlap sack.

I don't know how the others felt, but I didn't want to take the Sky Pilot in because he smelled and ate books and was obviously insane. Uncharitable of me, I know. But he also scared me, because that grip of his was frighteningly strong. Also, I hadn't been sleeping well, which made me irritable and subject to snappishness.

All the girls were looking at the ground, some with their arms folded. I imagine they were thinking of what having to take care of a smelly lunatic with religious delusions would do to their business. But the quiet and the guilt began to gnaw on me, and I was just about to give in and say to bring him to the agency, when Rose looked up and brushed the hair from her eyes.

"I will," she said.

"At the sporting house?" Doc asked.

"There's a store room," she said. "It will be all right."

"What about Miss Phossy?" April—or it might have been May—asked.

Miss Phossy was the madam at the China Doll, and she was one of the most feared characters in Dodge City; not only was she as mean as a snake, but she had a countenance to match.

"Miss Phossy owes me," Rose said. "It will be all right."

"Good girl," Doc said. "Send to Sturm's for a block of ice to be delivered, and make sure you chip it up fine. I'll bring the chamomile along directly."

"Thank you, Rose," I said, and handed over the cannibalized Bible.

As I walked back across the scorching street to my agency, I had an uneasy feeling that dogged my steps. I was glad that Rose had agreed to nurse the Sky Pilot, but there was something about him that disturbed me. There was a mystery growing here. It wasn't just that we didn't know his name or where he'd been; the biblical reference to ravens and the missing pages of Genesis were a bit more than odd, considering my situation. I'd been a detective who consults spirits for a little more than a year now, with a pet raven named Eddie and an infuriating partner named Jack Calder. If there was one thing I'd learned, it was that things in Dodge City aren't just stranger than they appear.

Things are stranger than you could imagine.

2

The unfortunate I would come to know as Molly Howart appeared at the door of the agency at four o'clock on Sunday afternoon, three days after the appearance of the Sky Pilot, her hands cupped around her bloodshot eyes, her red face flattened against the window—a perfectly pitiful apparition.

She startled me so that I dropped my pen.

The nib skittered and left a looping trail of black ink over the top of the oak desk, my papers, and the right cuff of my best white shirt.

"Fils de salope," I exclaimed. *Sonuvabitch.*

This alarmed the raven on his perch in the corner, atop the bookcase, and he squawked and beat his wings.

"Midnight visitor!" he croaked.

"Settle down, Eddie," I said. "She's real enough, and it's not even noon."

I crossed to the door and tapped the pasteboard sign. Calder & Wylde, Consulting Detectives, was closed. The woman, however, gave no indication that she understood. She remained rooted by the window, eyes downcast, hands clasped. Alarmed that she might be suffering some kind of spell, I unlocked the door and opened it a crack.

"Are you all right?"

"Miss Ophelia Wylde?"

"Are you in some distress?" I asked.

"A problem is causing me great discomfort," she said. "But it is a spiritual concern. I am in no immediate physical danger."

"Of that I am glad," I said, forcing a smile, "but the agency is quite closed. Do return during business hours."

"But you are Miss Wylde? The woman who talks to ghosts?"

"Yes, and I will be tomorrow as well," I said. "Come back then. But not too early, as I haven't been sleeping well."

I should have slammed the door, but the woman radiated sadness like a stove gives heat. Her weepy eyes looked at her own clasped hands, then to my hand upon the door, and finally to the stain on my sleeve. Her expression turned from sorrow to guilt.

"I've caused that stain," she said, talking more to herself than to me. "You'd better put something on it before it sets. I apologize and will cause you no more trouble today."

She turned to go.

"What would I use?" I asked.

She stopped.

"Pardon?"

"For the stain," I said, opening the door wide enough so that it touched, but did not ring, the announcing bell above it. "These domestic matters escape me. What would I use to keep it from setting?"

"Vinegar," she said. "Then warm water and soap."

I sighed.

"I have no vinegar," I said.

The afternoon seemed suddenly quite empty. Why would a lack of vinegar plunge me into a fit of melancholia? It wasn't the shirt, but what the stain on the white shirt represented, and that it was now permanent; that I lacked any of the essentials to create a home; that I was spending another Sunday afternoon alone, save for a talking bird; and that, in my hour of need, I was denied even the consolation of sour wine, a biblical resonance that is at once absurd and indicates the depth of my sudden self-pity.

"Come in, please," I said, opening the door and ringing the bell.

"No, I've already imposed."

"Do me the favor," I said. "I am in the mood for company."

While I sat behind the oak desk, the woman slumped in the cane chair opposite. She patted her hair with her hand and began her story, which she had obviously spent some time rehearsing.

"My name is Mary Howart," she said. "My friends call me Molly, and you may call me that as well, if you are a candidate for that position. My husband is Charles Howart, an employee of Morris Collar's railway freight business. We were married six years ago in Newton, and came to Dodge last year. We have a trim little house on Chestnut Street with two pear trees started in the front yard and a vegetable garden out back. Although the Lord has not seen fit to bless us with children, Charlie is a good and temperate man and attends services at least once a month with me at Union Church on Gospel Hill."

"Your life sounds pleasant enough," I said. "Why do you need my help?"

She hid her face with her hand, fingertips trembling on her forehead.

"Because," she said, in a voice so low that I had to lean forward to catch the words. "We are haunted by a book."

I considered this statement for a moment.

"Do you mean a book appears to you?"

"No, the book is real enough," Molly said. "It's just an ordinary book, but the way Charlie treats it, you'd think it was made out of gold. He frets over it, moving it from one hiding place to another in the house, even getting up in the middle of the night to check on it."

"What kind of book is it?"

"I told you, just an ordinary kind of book."

"Not a grimoire?"

She looked at me blankly.

"A book of witchcraft, of spells or curses?"

"No, nothing like that."

"The title, then?"

"There was once a title on the cover, in gilt, but most of the letters have been worn or rubbed away. What's left is an *S*, an *X*, and a *W*."

"It is a red book?"

"Yes, it is red leather."

"And the letters," I said. "You're quite sure?"

She repeated them: *S, X, W.*

"Do you know this book?" she asked.

"No," I said. "Can't say that I do, but I may have seen it once. Wish I could tell you where."

"The author's name is Gresham."

"Oh?"

"Yes, W. L. Gresham. It's on the spine."

I made a note—using a pencil.

"Have you read it?" I asked.

"Charlie never lets anyone read it—not even me. He keeps it wrapped up in an old flour sack, he says to keep the Kansas sand out of it, but I think it's really to hide it. I asked him about it once, and he said it was just a story . . . a kind of fable, I think that is the word he used."

"Did you ask him why he won't let you read it?"

"Because of the ghost," Molly said. "He says it has caused so much trouble already, that he can't stand the thought of what understanding the book might do to me."

"Curious," I said. "Has this been going on for all six years of your marriage?"

"No, only since April. It was then that Charlie

started acting jumpy and began constantly worrying where the book was. The ghost came the first time on the last Monday in April."

"Tell me about that."

"It was a quiet night, because you know it was too early in the season for the cattle drives to have reached Dodge yet. Charlie and I were both asleep when we heard the strangest sound coming from the parlor. A kind of mournful creaking, the protest of wood under strain, accompanied by the sighing of wind. We were afraid somebody was trying to break in, so Charlie jumped up and grabbed the shotgun he keeps in the corner, and he crept to the parlor. He kept telling me to stay put, but I was right behind him, looking over his shoulder."

"What did you see?"

"An unspeakable horror."

"If you could put this horror into words, what would they be?"

The woman thought for a moment.

"At first all I could see was some kind of bluish glow illuminating the parlor like a cold flame," she said. "It hovered and bobbed in the middle of the room about chest height, as if it were suspended from an unseen cord, accompanied by the sound of the wind and that awful creaking. I took it for a foxfire light, because when I was a child in Missouri I heard tales of lights such as this drifting through cemeteries. But this was the first time I had ever seen anything I was unable to identify as belonging to this world and not the next."

She paused.

"I wish it had been the last."

"Please, go on."

"The glow turned into a flame, and elongated, and took the shape of a pillar of fire with a brilliant star at the top. I told Charlie to fetch the Bible, but it was on a table on the opposite side of the room, and he was afraid to pass too close to the light," she said. "I was afraid as well. So we stood there, frozen, staring at this unearthly blue flame that gave no heat."

She looked down at her clasped hands.

"Then the pillar of flame began to take shape, resolving into a human form," she said. "It was a hanged man, eyes open and hard as marbles, his black tongue protruding from swollen lips. The veins in his neck were thick and looked like worms above the rope. His hands were free and hung limp at his sides, and the fingertips and thumbs were dark and engorged. The toes of his boots pointed earthward in slowly inscribing circles as he twisted from the ghostly rope."

"How awful," I offered.

"But I haven't told you the worst part," she said. "On the floor, beneath the hanged man, was the book. It was open and the pages were riffling in a breeze felt by no living person. Then, as the body turned on the rope to face us for perhaps the third time, the body stopped and the dead man's right hand came up and slowly pointed a dreadful forefinger."

"You must have been frightened."

"I was mortified," Molly said. "Charlie began to tremble."

She let out a burst of nervous laughter.

"I'm sorry," she said. "I shouldn't have said that. Charlie would be so embarrassed."

"Who could blame him?" I asked.

"He cried out like a little girl."

"Some do," I said.

"Have you?"

"Never," I said. "What happened next?"

"The apparition dissolved, leaving the parlor dark. The book, however, remained on the floor."

"Fascinating," I said. "What became of the book?"

"Charlie swept the cursed thing up and hid it, I know not where. By that time, I was on my knees, praying, eyes shut tight."

"Did you know the man?"

"No."

"Can you recollect any clues, in the manner of his dress, perhaps?"

"He was wearing the kind of western garb common some fifteen or twenty years ago, I suppose. A dark vest and checkered trousers. Oh, on the vest was pinned a note. It said, 'Here hangs a horse thief.'"

"You say the ghost came the first time in April," I said. "How many times has it appeared?"

"Every Monday night, at a few minutes after eleven."

"The same scene is repeated? The finger pointing?"

"And the book," Molly said. "No matter where Charlie hides it, it is always found open in the middle of the parlor floor."

"This is extraordinary," I said.

"I'm not sure that's the word I would use."

"I mean it is of note," I explained. "This is a haunting in which a physical object is compelled. I have heard of doors and windows opening by themselves, but never of objects being carried or somehow compelled to appear in a certain location. Has your husband removed the book from your home in an attempt to forestall these Monday visitations?"

"I suggested as much," Molly said. "But Charlie insists the book remain in the house, under his care."

"Then he is hiding something."

Molly recoiled as if wounded.

"The thought must have crossed your mind," I suggested.

She shook her head.

"Another woman?"

"No, he would never."

"Perhaps he is in debt, or in ill health . . ."

"Nothing like that. I would know."

"Has he done anything unusual or out of character in the last few weeks, apart from this business of the ghost and the book?"

Molly thought for a moment.

"He did buy an insurance policy," she said.

"With you as the beneficiary?"

"Yes," she said. "It was quite an expensive policy, worth five thousand dollars, and I told him we couldn't afford it, but he was adamant that I be taken care of in case something happened to him. This was a few weeks ago."

"About the time the apparition first appeared?"

"Yes," she said. "He brought the policy home and pressed it into my hand in a rather strange way. I still have it, in my bag."

"May I see it?"

The certificate was printed on good-quality paper with an elaborate fine-lined drawing of Athena with her shield, making it resemble a bond or a bank note. Scrolled across the top was *WESTERN MUTUAL LIFE ASSURANCE COMPANY OF LEAVENWORTH,* and in the right hand corner it said, *Policy No. 784.*

I handed back the policy.

"Where is he now?"

"At the Saratoga," she said. "He's been drinking some since the ghost first appeared. It eases his nerves, he says."

That can't be good for him, I thought.

"Have you shared this with anyone?" I asked.

"No," she said. "I've been afraid to."

A silence passed between us. Then, she asked, "Will you help me?"

"Yes, if you're willing to know the truth," I said. "You asked earlier if I talked to ghosts."

"That's what I read in the newspaper," she said. "The story of the murdered girl found on the Hundredth Meridian marker by the railroad tracks. You talked to that poor girl's ghost, and you and Mister Calder tracked her killer clear to Texas."

"I appreciate the publicity our friends at the *Dodge City Times* have given us," I said, "but the facts of what I have come to think of as the Case of Revenant No. 1, the Mystery of the Girl Betrayed, were somewhat different. There were certain details that were of necessity excluded from the newspaper account."

"Certain details?"

"It is true that the murder was solved in approximately the fashion the newspaper reported," I said. "There was, however, more to the climax of the adventure than the *Times* revealed. I have been working on my own account," I said, motioning to the papers. "It has proved more difficult than I anticipated, however."

"Writing down a story must be hard work."

"It's not the writing," I said. "It's telling the truth about oneself."

"You're not truthful?"

"I am now," I said. "But there was a long period in my life when I wasn't. I was a con woman, a shyster, a spook artist of the first order. I am ashamed of it now, but there's nothing I can do about it, except to make amends to those I've hurt, where possible."

Molly thought about this.

"Are you lying now about talking to ghosts?" she asked.

"Talking isn't the right word," I said. "Ghosts don't answer direct questions from the living, generally, but they do provide clues if you listen closely. Ghosts never lie, but demons often do. Not all the dead manifest as ghosts, but when they do it's because of unfinished business, and they can only pass over when that business is resolved."

"What is your rate?"

"My fee is twenty dollars, payable in advance, for a week's detection," I said, reciting from memory the lines I had spent hours composing. "That amount includes the assistance of Mister Calder, if needed, but it does not include travel or other expenses. These expenses will be subject to your approval before they are incurred and will be itemized and due upon completion of the case."

"This all sounds so businesslike."

"It is a business," I said. "Ghosts may not require food or heat or a roof over their heads, but human beings do, as my partner is constantly reminding me. I am just as deserving of compensation as any of the other tradesmen along Front Street who provide a service. And so my clients know this is not some kind of swindle, all monies, save expenses, of course, will be returned if the mystery is not satisfactorily explained."

"Oh, I didn't mean that," she said. "It just seems so strange, dealing with spirits in such a dollars and cents way. You have done this a lot since the Russian girl?"

"More than a few times," I said. "Yours would be Revenant No. 15."

"These cases were successes?"

"For the most part," I said. "Many common noisy ghosts, with no mystery to be solved. One will-o'-the-wisp. The murder of a drover by his partner, and the resulting haunting of said partner. Three ghosts with family secrets to convey. Another unhappy that his grave remained unmarked after six months. They all crossed over quickly, once their business was finished."

"Are you occupied tomorrow night?"

"I am now," I said.

Molly Howart opened her clutch and counted out twenty dollars in single greenbacks. She placed the pile of notes carefully on the desk, atop the ink-stained manuscript.

I stared at the money.

"Isn't that the correct sum?" she asked.

"Yes, it's perfect," I said.

I could feel myself blush, a warm feeling that spread across my neck and cheeks and settled burning in my earlobes. Slowly, I pushed the money back across the table.

"I'm sorry, it slipped my mind that my partner, Mister Calder, has the books with him just now, so I am unable to write you a receipt. Do you mind holding my fee until, well, later?"

She nodded and returned the money to her clutch.

"May I ask a final question?"

I said it would be all right.

"Where do we go when we die?"

"I don't know where we go when we die," I said, "but I know how we get there, because I saw it last night in my dreams. We take the train."

3

It's a scorching night in midsummer, the sky is shot with stars, and I'm standing on the depot platform at Dodge City in what might be a wedding dress. I can see the headlight of a train as it shimmies up the tracks far to the east, but I don't hear the familiar locomotive rumble.

There is no sound from the train at all.

This is when I notice the platform is deserted and the depot windows are dark. I have no bags, not even a valise, and I'm vaguely confused because Eddie isn't on my shoulder and I don't see his cage anywhere. At this point, I suspect I'm dreaming, but if there's a reason to wake myself up, I am unable to articulate the thought.

I glance back to the city, and North Front Street is roaring like a prairie fire, with Texans and other wildlife stampeding from one watering hole to the next. There's the plink of pianos and the cry of fiddles punctuated by drunken laughter. I look up at my corner room at the Dodge House, Room 217, but the windows are dark and the curtains drawn.

As the train nears, sparks fountain from the stack and the firebox casts a hellish light on the railway bed. The engine is short and squat, and the headlight is mounted off center, a design I've never seen before, but which seems familiar still. The train has seven cars, including a baggage car, and a mysterious car draped in black at the end instead of a caboose.

The spectral train comes to a silent stop, with clouds of steam enveloping the platform. I'm standing now in front of the first passenger car, and I can see the inside is filled with an unearthly blue light. I want to climb inside the car, but I'm afraid. I glance down the platform and see dark figures wheeling up a baggage cart to the side of the express car.

A coffin is lifted into the car by shadowy hands.

"All aboard, miss."

The conductor beckons from the steps of the passenger car. He is a kindly old gentleman, of a type often found in books for children, and he wears a blue uniform with gold buttons and a smart-looking cap.

"I don't have a ticket," I say.

"Oh, you don't need one. Your passage has already been arranged."

The conductor offers a gloved hand and helps me into the car. As soon as I'm inside, the train begins to glide away from the station.

"Where are we going?"

"The end of the line, of course," the conductor says.

"How far is that?"

"Really can't say."

The train is picking up some speed now. The dark

prairie rushes past the windows, and I can see the glint of starlight from water.

"Is that the Arkansas River?"

"No," the conductor says. "It's the Acheron."

"I'm in hell, then."

"We haven't crossed it yet."

I ask if we will cross, and the conductor demurs.

"If I don't know where I'm bound, what am I doing here?"

The conductor produces a ticket from his vest pocket and hands it to me. It is like a standard railway ticket, but has the number 000. There is printing on the ticket, but as usual in dreams, I can't read it.

"What is this?"

"Your temporary pass," the conductor says. "Regular passengers are assigned consecutively numbered tickets. Special guests are given these unnumbered ones. Mind that you don't lose it."

I clutch the ticket tightly in my hand.

"You'd better hurry, miss," he says, pointing to the back of the train. "You are expected."

I start down the aisle, passing a decidedly democratic collection of humanity in the seats along either side. There are men and women of all ages, and children, and their clothing ranges from that of wretches to the upper classes, but the majority appear to be working, or working poor. There seem a disproportionate number of babies on board, but none is crying.

As I step between the cars, I am made dizzy by the rush of the wind. I grasp the rail to steady myself but make the mistake of looking down. We are crossing a rugged canyon on an improbably high bridge, and for a moment I am frozen with fear. It's not that I'm afraid I'm going to fall.

I'm afraid I'll jump.

"What's wrong with you, Ophelia?"

It's a familiar voice, and I look up to see Jack Calder standing in the vestibule of the next car.

"Oh, Jack," I say. "What are you doing here?"

Calder dismisses my question with a laugh. Then he reaches out and grabs my right wrist and pulls me roughly into the car—and tightly against him. He's wearing his favorite blue shirt and a leather vest, but there's no heavy gun belt between us.

"Are you dead, too?" I ask.

"Don't be so dramatic," Calder says. "I'm going to hell, for the things I've done on the Vigilance Committee, but it's not my time yet. When it is, you'll know it."

Then Calder is gone, and I have suddenly passed through all of the passenger cars to what I thought was the baggage car, but now I see that it is a kind of railway hearse, with racks on each side hung with funeral drapery. There's twenty-four coffins and caskets (I can always count and decipher numbers in dreams, but never words), and as I pass among them I come to the plain wooden coffin I saw being loaded at Dodge.

Shadows flit around the coffin, implike figures that have the substance of smoke. One of the things has a very solid-looking carpenter's brace and bit, and is quickly removing the screws securing the coffin lid. I flinch as the top falls away, half-expecting to see myself in the box.

The imps laugh and point at me.

Inside the coffin is a stranger, a man of middle age

with a purple face and a rope around his neck. As the imps begin to tug at the knot to loosen the rope, the dead man's eyes open.

I walk on.

Then I pass into the last car, a richly appointed private car fit for, well, a Commodore Vanderbilt. Everything that isn't walnut is black or purple. There are plush chairs everywhere, and silver table service, and crystal decanters filled with expensive-looking liquor. There are even pieces of art. There is a marble bust of Alexander the Great, the Waterhouse painting of the Lady of Shalott, and a frightening gold and ebony statue of jackal-headed Anubis.

It's all so rich that I wouldn't be surprised to meet dead old Cornelius himself, considering he left a hundred million dollars behind when he went. But instead of a randy old man with wild hair, I encounter instead a strange figure dressed in black.

The figure stands behind an officious desk piled with newspaper obituaries, and next to the desk is a gold-plated telegraph machine that suddenly emits a burst of noisome clicks. The figure listens to the chatter, then leans over to make notes in a ledger with a gold-nibbed pen.

"Sit, please." A British accent.

I take a seat and examine my host. Skin as white as Alexander and eyes black like Anubis. Bald as poor Yorick. A heavy black robe is gathered at the waist by a gold sash.

"Are you a demon?"

"Of course not," he says impatiently.

I am uncertain of its gender, but for convenience I will use the masculine.

"Where's Eddie?"

"I think it strange that you have a raven for a companion," he says. "All this Poe business is overdone, don't you think? If birds could talk, don't you think they'd make better conversation? But then, you were raised by books. Byron and the rest of that Romantic trash."

He puts the pen in the well and rubs a hand across those black eyes with no pupils. I notice also that he has no eyebrows, which is oddly even more disconcerting.

"The bird is not here," he says. "Animals have their own line, over which I have no power."

"What about those things in the coffin car?"

"Subordinates," he says.

"They look like imps. Death imps."

"They certainly aren't imps, which are malevolent and chaotically disruptive," he says, clearly annoyed. "We call them widdershins, and they are helpful, if a bit disorganized."

"Widdershins?"

"Yes, for they are sinister to human eyes, portends of grave misfortune or disaster, a shadow that is glimpsed from the corner of a mortal's eye, but always moving to the left, always out of sight. It's all in the staff manual."

He taps the ledger.

"More books," I say. "Suddenly, I'm drowning in books. You used the plural. Who else does 'we' refer to?"

He holds up a hand.

"Questions! Such questions," he says. "Why are you so curious? Special passengers are typically quite docile."

"Why?"

"They are asleep, of course."

"I've had some practice at this sort of thing."

"Ah, that's what I want to discuss with you," he says.

He comes around the desk and drags a chair up to mine. Our knees are nearly touching. He leans forward, makes a tent of his fingers, and stares deeply into my face. Then he nods, as if he has solved some mystery, and flings himself back in the seat.

"You can see the type of operation we have here," he says, motioning about. "We perform a necessary service and things run smoothly, as a rule. It would be unfortunate if you were allowed to interfere with that. The company greatly appreciates your cooperation in this matter."

He smiles.

"Thank you, that's all."

"You're Death, then."

Death smiles.

"I prefer the term superintendent. We've had a pleasant chat, haven't we? Now, off with you. There's a good woman."

His voice is so soothing that I stand and smile and am about to thank him for his time when a growing sense of unfairness makes me turn and wag my finger in Death's face.

"How, exactly, am I interfering?"

Death folds his marble hands over his stomach.

"You communicate with the dead."

"And what's wrong with that?"

"You're infringing on my territory."

"It is what I'm meant to do," I say.

"We have an entire department assigned to it," Death says. "Do you think the spiritual telegraph was invented yesterday? Why, name just about any evidence of high concept of other-worldly communication, from Jacob's ladder to the sewing machine, and that's our work."

"The sewing machine?"

"Came to Elias Howe in a dream. Changed everything."

"All of that is very unlike what I do," I say. "I don't dream inventions for others, I don't deliver prophecies, I claim no market on revealed truth. I listen to the dead and help them cross over, when I can. That's it."

Death shakes his head.

"These things never turn out well," he says. "The Greeks and all that. Too much of a temptation to meddle. Most human beings find it slightly distasteful, at any rate. The age of the Nekromanteion is over. Why should the living have any truck with the dead, anyway? I'm sure you'll be happier being a normal sort of person."

"Now there's something to think about."

"Yes, normal."

"No, I meant happy. Is it possible?"

"Well, as I understand it, for some."

"For normal sorts."

"Well, yes."

"If I were the normal sort, would I be here talking to you?"

"Point taken, Miss Wylde."

"I'm just as mad as the Sky Pilot, aren't I?"

"All human beings are mad," Death says. "But the man you refer to as the Sky Pilot is merely ill, a vari-

*ant of the well-known Jerusalem syndrome. There's
something about deserts and other empty spaces that can
trigger religious mania in some. There isn't a name for
his malady as yet, but I hear the authorities are leaning toward Prairie Passion. Personally, I find the allit-
eration unfortunate, and would prefer something else.
Kansas Fever, perhaps. John Brown and all that . . ."*

"Will he get better?"

"His name is Martin."

"Truly?"

"You really must stop asking questions," he says.

"You're Death," I say. "Don't you have the power to
stop me?"

"That would violate the free will clause of the charter."

I laugh.

"Is any of this real?"

"It is uniquely real," Death says. "The mode of transportation changes every now and again, but never the
method. Personally, I'm glad we're done with boats.
And horses. What a mess! Oh, some of our branch offices still use horse-drawn hearses, but everything is
up to date here at transportation headquarters. For you
and millions of others, a train will carry you over to
your final destination. In your case . . . well, this is the
actual train."

"Not a ghost train."

"Well, it is in spectral form now, of course," Death
says, pride growing in his voice. "And this business of
describing our operation is couched in terms you will
find familiar. But this is the train, outfitted the way you
will see it when your time comes."

4

Then I woke, before dawn on the day after Molly Howart came to see me, with my heart pounding and in a knot of damp sheets. *Who really wants to know when they're going to die?* I asked myself.

Apparently, I did.

It was still dark and I untangled myself from the sheets and crawled out of bed and stood for a moment, so frightened that I was shaking. My throat was dry and my head ached. I went to the dressing table and felt for the pitcher and nearly knocked it over, but caught it before it spilled, and used both hands to bring it to my mouth and drank desperately. Eddie, disturbed by my clanking and slurping, made a weak cry of protest.

"Sorry," I said. "Nighttime is for sleeping."

Then I heard laughing.

I had forgotten to throw a sheet over the mirror on the table before going to sleep. A greenish glow emanated from inside the glass, where a ghostly face regarded me with amusement.

"Shut up, Hank," I said.

"You shot up like a jack-in-the-box. It was funny."

The apparition's name was Horrible Hank and he'd been with me, more or less, since childhood. He'd been a mud clerk on the steamboat *Pennsylvania* and had sustained a fatal wound when its boiler exploded, when the steamer was just below Memphis, in 1858. He had formed some odd affection for me because of some small kindness I showed him and his distraught brother as he lay near death, which might explain why I was the only one who could see him. He wasn't a usual ghost, but more of a type of noisy ghost that had attached himself to me alone, and one of the few otherworldly things I could have a two-way conversation with.

"It wasn't funny to me, Hank," I said, annoyed. "Why aren't you ready to cross over?"

Hank shrugged. His hair and clothing were blasted by some gale-force wind on his side of the mirror.

"Guess I'm having too much fun here."

"Well, you're disturbing," I said. "Someday, I'm going to find a way to get rid of you."

"You'd miss me, sweetheart," he said.

"I'd like to try that theory out. I'm thinking of getting rid of all my mirrors."

"With that tangle you call a head of hair, I wouldn't advise it," he said. "Besides, you can't get rid of all reflections. There's windowpanes, glasses of water, polished metal . . ."

"Hank, do you think dreams are real?"

"How should I know?" he asked. "My world is a bit . . . limited."

"Just once, I wish you could give me some useful piece of information. Do you know anything about ghost trains?"

"No."

"What about a red book?"

"Don't know what you're talking about," he said. "Is that something my brother has written?"

"No," I said. "Just something from my dreams."

"Hey, I've got a joke about dreams for you."

"Please, no."

"One day a little boy woke up and told his mother that he had dreamed that his grandfather had died and, lo and behold, that afternoon the family received word that the poor old man had indeed shuffled the mortal coil."

"Hank," I said sternly.

"The next night the little boy dreamed that the neighbor's dog was run over by a team of horses and, lo and behold, that exact thing happened. The family was astonished."

"Lord, spare me."

"Then, on the third night, the boy had a dream that his father dropped dead. The family was naturally distraught, so every precaution was taken to keep the father safe from harm. He stayed in bed all day, not even rising to wash or shave himself, and he ate nothing for fear of choking. The other family members stood watch at his door, and allowed no one inside to guard against evil intent. And then . . ."

He stopped.

"Are you listening?" he asked.

"Yes," I said. "Finish it, quickly."

"And then a drummer came to the house, and fell dead on the steps."

5

I was fully awake now, so I walked over to look out the window at the street below. It was still full dark out, and hot, with no hint of dawn, but it must have been early morning because North Front Street was just about shut down. The only lights were from the windows of the scattered restaurants that had opened to feed drunken cowboys and prepare for the regular breakfast crowd.

Afraid to go back to sleep, I pulled on my clothes as quietly as I could, but Eddie still fussed. Downstairs, the Dodge House was quiet as a church, and even the desk clerk was asleep at his post. I went out into the hot night air and walked down the hard-packed dirt street to Beatty and Kelly's Restaurant, where I took a table near the kitchen and asked for a cup of coffee.

"So, you've had enough whiskey for one night."

The waiter was a young man with dark, slicked-back hair and a towel thrown over his shoulder. He seemed annoyingly alert for so early in the morning, and the way he looked at me made me feel small.

"I don't drink," I said.

"Of course not, sweetheart," the waiter said. "I've quit a thousand times myself. You want breakfast? We have eggs, but no biscuits yet. And steak. We always have steak, any way you like it. Porterhouse, sirloin, flank. Medium, well done, or raw."

"This is a cattle town," I said.

"Let me order you up a steak," he said. "You look a tad anemic. And if you don't mind me saying so, the men's clothing is not showing your figure to best advantage. There are some girls who carry it well, but they are generally more ample. I do like your red hair, though."

"Excuse me, but do I know you?" I asked. "Have we met and I just don't remember? Your remarks are unwelcome, and I can assure you that I do not dress to a calculated advantage."

"Sorry," he said. "I usually get along well with the girls. No, we've not met before. All business, I understand. My name is Bernard, by the way. So, coffee only?"

"Yes, coffee," I said. "What time is it?"

"Coming up on four, I think."

Another hour to dawn.

Somebody had left Saturday's edition of the *Dodge City Times* on the table. Bored, I glanced at the front page. There was a story about the thousand Cheyenne Indians being transferred from the Red Cloud Agency in the Dakotas to Indian Territory by the U.S. Army, and who were expected to arrive near Dodge in a few days; an item about the war between the Turks and the Russians; and a perfectly awful poem entitled, "The Last of Summer."

There was a paid notice at the bottom left of the front page, in the "Professional Cards" section, which carried notices for stray cattle, itinerant photographers, law and collections, and the like. The ad that caught my eye was headed, "THE GREATEST POSSIBLE PROTECTION FROM THE DEADLY WHEEL," in bold type, and claimed the policies offered by the Western Mutual Life Assurance Company of Leavenworth pay for the loss of a thumb, or a forefinger, a hand, a foot, or the loss of sight in one or both eyes. A representative of the company would be in town for one week only, and that those interested in obtaining ultimate security could call at the Dodge House. "BUY THE BEST. BUILD THE WEST."

The advertisement caused me to make a small sound of disgust in my throat, and I quickly flipped the page. Insurance salesmen struck me as a sinister brotherhood dedicated to accosting innocents on the street and interrupting one's dinner hour to shill for a lottery that you only won if you lost.

Inside, there was a long story taken from one of the New York papers about the faith and practices of the Mohammedans; an item about a $17 million contract Turkey had taken out with the Providence Tool Company, for hundreds of thousands of Martini-Henry rifles, the biggest contract ever made in this country by a foreign government; and a paragraph in the personal news column about a former lawman returning to town.

> Wyatt Earp, who was on our city police force last summer, is in town again. We hope he will accept a position on the force once more. He had a quiet way of taking the most desperate characters into custody. . . . It wasn't considered polite to draw a gun on Wyatt unless you got the drop and meant to burn powder without any preliminary talk.

I drank the coffee my wide-awake waiter, Bernard, had brought, and flipped through the rest of the eight-page paper. There was a letter reprinted from a Robert Creuzbaur of Brooklyn to *The New York Sun* defending the practice of dowsing.

"I wish to draw attention to the useful purposes the rod can serve," Creuzbaur wrote, "and particularly to the points which science might take hold of to solve other questions in the mysterious field of electricity, to which I ascribe the rod's action."

Creuzbaur, who claimed to have long used a divining rod to locate water for digging wells, said that a recent article in a scientific journal had maligned dowsing by ascribing it to the realm of superstition. Electricity, he said, must be the key by which the rod works, because placing a pane of glass or a silk handkerchief beneath the tip of the rod prevents the desired action.

"The ban of superstition being once removed from this subject," Creuzbaur wrote, "when leading minds in the science of electricity shall have recognized it as worthy of their attention, an important advance in the knowledge of that invisible and all-powerful factor of Creation is not unlikely to be arrived at."

There was another story, on the page opposite the dowsing story, about the upcoming trial of a "spirit photographer" in Denver. The photographer, Eureka Smith, was accused of defrauding several prominent clients—including the wife of gubernatorial candidate Andrew Jackson Miles—by using fakery to produce photographic portraits that purported to show dead relatives hovering behind the living.

"Noted Daguerreotypist and spirit skeptic Abraham Bogardus, of Philadelphia, has been retained by the prosecution to demonstrate the methods by which these so-called 'spirit photographs' can be produced at will," the newspaper reported. "Attorney General Sampson has claimed in his indictment that defendant Smith has bilked hundreds of dollars from grieving families desperate for proof of the survival of their lost loved ones. In at least one instance, the attorney general charged, Smith had also produced humbuggery aimed at extorting money from a prominent city politician."

I knew Bogardus by reputation, considering my past vocation. Bogardus had testified at the 1869 trial of William H. Mumler, whose most famous spirit photograph was of Mary Todd Lincoln with the ghost of Abraham Lincoln behind her, his hands on her shoulders. Mumler was accused by P. T. Barnum (who apparently wanted to keep hucksterism all to himself) and others of fraud, and Bogardus demonstrated the ease with which spirit photographs could be faked. A journalist by the name of Moses Dow, however, testified that he had investigated Mumler's technique and could find no trace of trickery. Although acquitted of fraud, Mumler's reputation was ruined, and he was driven to the poor house.

"Can't recall seeing you out and about this early before."

Jack Calder sat down at the table.

"Couldn't sleep," I said, dropping the paper. "Nightmare."

"To be expected, in your line of work."

"It's *our* line of work," I said. "We're partners, remember?"

"Sure, but you handle the spook end of it," he said. "And I handle the bill-paying end."

"I'm sorry, Jack."

"If it wasn't for me writing bail bonds, serving papers, and bringing back jumpers, we'd have gone out of business in April."

I felt guilty. Just a year before, I had settled a

considerable debt from my previous career, and had two hundred dollars left with which to help establish the agency. But everything had been more expensive than I had expected, from the lettering of the sign on the door to the oil for the lanterns.

"I'm sure things will pick up soon," I said. "Business runs in cycles, that's what I've heard."

"We have business," Calder said. "You're going to have to start charging, Ophelia."

I looked at the table.

"It's difficult for me," I said. "It's not as easy as when I was, you know."

"A confidence woman."

"Yes, Jack. It's much harder than that."

"What was the nightmare about?" he asked.

"Something about a train."

He looked at me as if he expected more, but I wasn't inclined to indulge him.

"Are you always up this early?" I asked.

"Most days," he said. "Got to get things done while it's still cool enough to work."

Calder was wearing the blue shirt and vest, and slung around his waist was his cartridge belt with the pistol that looked as big as a blacksmith's hammer. It was illegal to carry guns north of the deadline in Dodge City, but Calder was exempt because he was a bounty hunter, and was considered an extension of the court.

"Hello, Jack," Bernard said, suddenly appearing at the table. He placed a cup of coffee and a sugar bowl and spoon on the table.

"Good morning, Bernard," Calder said, spooning sugar into his coffee. He put three heaping spoonfuls into the coffee, then stirred with vigor, the bowl of the spoon clicking and scraping irritatingly against the sides of the cup.

"Be careful sitting with this one," Bernard said, inclining his head toward me. "She's in a not very good mood."

"Good advice," Calder said, then smiled at me. "Thanks."

"The usual this morning?"

"Sounds about right," Calder said. He placed a calloused forefinger through the ceramic handle and brought the mug to his lips. I thought the coffee must taste about like molasses, considering the amount of sugar he used.

After Bernard had walked away, Calder leaned back in his chair and gave me a knowing grin.

"What's so funny?"

"Bernie thinks you're a Cyprian."

"Whatever gave him that idea?"

"They don't get a lot of business here from unaccompanied women at four o'clock in the morning who aren't prostitutes," Calder said. "Bernie is friends with all of them."

"Merde."

"Cuss in English, will you?"

"I most certainly will not," I said. "I think in English and cuss in French and Creole."

"At least tell me what it means."

I wasn't going to give Calder the satisfaction

of knowing it was the most basic of scatological expressions.

"What do you know about a couple named Charles and Mary Howart?" I asked.

Calder shrugged.

"There's not much to know," he said. "Charlie keeps to himself, is a bookkeeper for the Collar freight company, I think. Drinks little and gambles less. Molly is a quiet woman who attends Union Church. They live on Chestnut and have no children. They're the kind of people anybody would want for neighbors—reliable, quiet, and a little dull."

"Things apparently have gotten more interesting for the Howarts," I said. "A haunted book is giving them trouble, every Monday night for the last few weeks. At least, that's what Molly described when she hired me. She asked me to come see for myself."

"What manner of haunted book?"

"A book bound in red Moroccan leather, written by a man named Gresham," I said. "Molly hasn't been allowed to read it and doesn't know the title. Charlie has had the book for several years, but of late the book has been manifesting a ghastly hanged man in their front room. Can you think of any reason this would be happening now?"

Calder shook his head.

"Perhaps I'll learn something Monday night," I said. "At least, I hope to get my hands on that book."

Bernard the waiter brought Calder a platter of

sirloin steak and scrambled eggs, and refilled both coffees. Calder asked if I wanted something, and I told him it was too early to even think about food.

"You're eating with a purpose," I said. "In a hurry?"

"I have paper on a couple of whiskey traders over on the Medicine Lodge River in Kiowa County," he said. "I aim to serve them before noon."

"Paper?" I asked. "Arrest warrants?"

"They're bail jumpers," Calder said. "They've already been arrested once. I'm going to bring their sorry hides back here to stand trial or know the reason why."

"Be careful, Jack," I said.

"These boys have no stomach for trouble," Calder said. "One of them is a Texan named Harker, and he's been on the drift for months. He used to be a cowhand but got tangled up here in Dodge with this other fellow, Smilin' Solomon Stone. They've been up to general disorder ever since. Some time in jail might be corrective. And a good beating."

"Jack," I said. "Are you still a member of the Vigilance Committee?"

He took a sip of his coffee, then cleared his throat.

"Why do you ask?"

"I had a dream," I said. "It came up."

"The committee hasn't met regular in a long while," he said.

"It might as well meet every Sunday, considering the reputation it still has in this town," I said. "Children aren't afraid of the bogeyman in Dodge City if they're bad, they're afraid of the Committee of Vigilance."

"Then I guess they'd better be good."

"Jack, I'm serious. What haven't you told me?"

"Ophelia," Calder said, then wiped his mouth with a checkered napkin. "I had a wife. She died. I don't need another."

Calder tossed the cloth on the table.

My cheeks blazed and I blinked back tears. I felt both ashamed and outraged, with more than a dash of betrayal thrown in. Why was he treating me this way?

"That was mean, Jack."

Calder pushed his half-eaten breakfast away and tossed a dollar note on the table.

"I thought we were partners."

He stood.

"That's it? You're not going to talk about this?"

"If I can find Harker and Stone, I should be back by dark," he said, avoiding my eyes. "But if I have to scare them up out of the brush, it may take a day or two. Longer, if they decide to run for Texas."

6

After Calder left, I sat at the table and drank more coffee and pondered what I had done to make him so cold to me. The prouder the man, the harder it is to get him to talk about his feelings. It was infuriating. We were supposed to be partners, and all I did was ask an honest question out of concern, and he treated me like I had killed his dog.

Then the front door banged open so hard I thought it was going to break the glass, and into the restaurant stumbled a local prostitute by the name of Frankie Bell. Everybody in Dodge City knew Frankie, or knew of her, because she did things that inspired gossip. For one, she was a whore and unashamed of it. This was undisturbing to the night denizens, but unacceptable to those who had daytime jobs, attended city council meetings, and went to church on Sundays. For another, she was a big girl—taller than most men, in fact, in her bare feet—and she had muscles under those curves, and she wasn't afraid to use them when she believed her honor had been challenged. Last week, she had pummeled a shoe salesman from Wichita who had suggested Frankie could turn a better profit as a circus curiosity.

"The usual, doll?" Bernard asked.

"Yep," Frankie said.

She was wearing a red kimono, her wild blond hair spilled over her shoulders, and a badly rolled cigarette dangled from her lower lip. Her brown eyes were bright with whiskey and she navigated the restaurant by gripping the backs of chairs like they were the rail on a storm-tossed ship. She found a table she liked by the kitchen door and sprawled in a chair.

Bernard brought a short glass and an armload of ingredients. In something resembling a ritual, he placed the glass in front of her, then cracked a raw egg on the rim, and plopped the unbroken yolk in. He poured about a shot from a bottle of Worcestershire sauce, added five shakes of Tabasco, and sprinkled it all with salt and pepper.

"It is ready," Bernard said.

Frankie nodded, snubbed the cigarette out on the tabletop, and snatched up the concoction in her right hand. She held the glass high and offered a toast in a surprisingly firm voice.

"Let those who did not get us cry," she said. "And let those who did not want us . . . muck off and die."

She threw the contents down her throat, wiped

her mouth with her forearm, and slammed the glass upside down on the table. The restaurant applauded, and Frankie nodded in appreciation.

"What was that?" I asked Bernard as he walked by with the empty glass.

"Prairie oyster," he said. "Want to try one?"

"Thanks, but I'll pass."

"Say, you're that Wylde gal who talks to ghosts," Frankie said, casting her wild eyes upon me. "What in hell did you do to old Hickory Lane?"

"I'm not sure what you mean."

"She's got it in for you something fierce."

"Oh?"

"She went on a drunk last night and said you were full of it."

"Did she, now?"

"Swore she was going to take you down a peg or two."

"I don't know why Hickory would feel that way about me, but I'm sure it's all a misunderstanding," I said.

Frankie snorted.

"The last person Hickory misunderstood," she said, "ended up losing her front teeth."

I turned away from Frankie Bell.

Through the restaurant windows, I could see people moving along Front Street, people with purpose, with lists of things to do. They were going to open stores for business, doing the shopping, paying bills, and settling accounts.

Dodge City was like that. By day, it was as normal as any little town you could hope for. By night, it was Sodom, Port Royal, and Deadwood all rolled into one.

I decided I might visit the *Times* office and quiz the Shinn brothers on the finer points of composition. But it was still only five o'clock in the morning and, having known journalists in other locales, I doubted the Shinns were likely to receive visitors much before ten or eleven o'clock, depending on how much inspiration they had drunk the night before. I decided instead to take a walk down by the river, while it was still cool enough to enjoy it.

I walked down to Bridge Street, crossed the Santa Fe tracks, and then ambled down to the sandy banks of the Arkansas a block or so east of the toll bridge. The river was low, just a few inches of water, but it was wide enough to brilliantly reflect the sunrise.

Looking at the dull orange ball of the sun through the trees, I thought about the heat that would surely come. Stepping down to the water's edge, I knelt on a broad, flat rock. The water was sluggish and fouled from the thousands of cattle nearby. The animals were either held in the railway pens in town, awaiting shipment, or in massive herds up and down the river, waiting for their turn to be driven into the city.

I popped off the celluloid collar of my shirt so I could feel the cool morning breeze against my throat. Then I undid my shirt a couple of buttons and loosened my vest. The wind stirred the cottonwoods and tall grass along the bank, and it made such a pleasant sound I closed my eyes, momentarily at peace.

The tranquility was disturbed by the sound of boots on gravel.

I opened my eyes. A tall man with long auburn hair walked toward me, whistling an old tune, and as he walked his hair swayed from side to side. He wore a paisley vest over a loose-fitting pink shirt with sleeves rolled up to the elbows. His denims were tucked into calf-length walking boots. Over his left shoulder was slung a well-worn brown leather satchel, of the kind used by troops during the war to carry their ammunition.

I stood and, turning my back, quickly buttoned my shirt.

"Pardon," he said. "Didn't know you were doing your business."

"You may have caught me at a disadvantage," I said. "But I was doing no business of any kind. I thank you to move on."

"Why don't you piss up a . . ." The man lost his thought and stared intently at my torso, and then up to my face. ". . . rope. By God, you're a woman."

"Of course I am."

"Forgive me, I just caught a glimpse of you and thought, naturally, because of your clothing, that you were a gentleman." His voice was soft and strongly British.

"That is something we must share."

"Pardon?"

"Being mistaken for the opposite gender," I said.

"Your hair goes below your shoulder blades. From the back, you must often be mistaken for a woman."

I was immediately sorry I had said it, because in truth I am attracted to well-groomed long hair in men, but I had wanted to hurt him. He gave no sign that he was at all sensitive about the matter, however.

"Pardon, but are you all right?"

"I'm sure it's no concern of yours," I said, both appalled and a little frightened by his rudeness. "Additionally, that isn't the kind of question one expects from a gentleman."

"Meant no offense," he said, brushing the hair out of his eyes. "But neither of us is the type of gentleman anybody would be expecting."

He reached casually down and retrieved my collar from where I had dropped it, offering it to me with a smile. I plucked it from his hand and shoved it into my pocket.

"Thank you," I said, meaning the opposite.

He reached into the satchel, and I must have flinched or otherwise telegraphed my concern, because he paused.

"I am disarmed," he said.

"Unarmed, you mean."

"No," he said. "I am disarmed by your beauty."

"Distracted, perhaps," I said. "Disarmed? Surely not."

From his satchel he removed a briar pipe with a straight stem and a pocket tin of Turkish tobacco. As he carefully filled the bowl of the pipe and tamped it with his thumb, he looked out over the water and squinted. His blue eyes reflected the dawn.

"I grew up on the bank of a river," he said. "Now I find comfort in walking a riverbank in the still of the mornings, even along rivers as small as this. It seems strange to me now, because when I was a boy I couldn't wait to leave the river behind."

He struck a wooden match on his belt buckle and fired the pipe. He sucked vigorously for a moment, then released a great cloud of smoke.

"Let's start over, shall we?"

I was silent for a few moments.

"What river?" I asked.

"The Thames," he said. "A neighborhood called Millwall, on the west side of the Isle of Dogs. Not an island, really, but a peninsula the river loops around. Home to builders of ships and barges and ironworks of great import."

"Were you a shipbuilder, or a sailor?"

"Good heavens, no," he said, the stem of the pipe clicking against his teeth. "I was a mudlark, as was my father before me. Ah, I see by your expression you don't know the term, but then I wouldn't expect anyone outside of England to recognize it. Mudlarks claw a living from the banks of the river, scavenging whatever has fallen from the great ships that pass: chunks of coal, iron rivets and washers, bits of rope and canvas. Working in the filth and muck from first light until full dark. On a good day you might earn a few pence. Other days, only a farthing."

He shook his head.

"I forget myself," he said. "I have disturbed your morning meditation with melancholy ramblings about a time long ago and dead. It is inappropriate for a man of common stock to share intimate conversation with a gentlewoman to whom he has not been properly introduced."

I told him I didn't mind strangers sharing stories, as long as they proved interesting. He said if I would share my name, then we would no longer be strangers.

"My name is Ophelia," I said.

He smiled.

"Your name suits you," he said. "I was never comfortable with mine. It hung like a stone around my neck growing up: Bithersea. I am the son of a Bithersea, who was the son of a Bithersea, who was the . . . Wouldn't it be grand if we could choose our own names, when we come of age, instead of being branded at birth like a twist of tobacco or a box of soap?"

"What is your Christian name?"

"Bryce."

"Charmed."

"As am I, Ophelia. And your last name?"

"Wylde."

"Of course it is, Miss Wylde."

"And what do they call you here in the states?"

"Chatwin," he said. "Bruce Chatwin. It sounds

ever so much better than Bryce Bithersea, don't you think?"

"It does have a certain ring to it," I allowed. "Tell me, Bruce, because I have no head for British money. How much is a farthing?"

"It takes four farthings to make a penny," Chatwin said.

I asked him when his occupation as a mudlark came to an end.

"When I stowed away on one of those great ships and came to America," he said. "I was thirteen years old and landed in Five Points in New York, which was like jumping from purgatory straight to hell. Even the Irish gangs wouldn't have me, at least not until I learned their cant and proved myself."

"And how did you do that?"

"I made myself useful, don't you know?"

"No, I don't."

He took the pipe out of his mouth and frowned at the bowl, which had grown cold.

"I never killed," he said. "And I never hurt a child or a woman. But I gave plenty of pain to men."

Chatwin tapped out the contents of the pipe against his heel.

"So, you were a criminal."

"A minor one, yes."

"People sometimes change," I said. "How did you get out of New York?"

"The draft," he said. "In 1863, a rich man paid me to take the place of his son in the Union

Army. I deserted the first chance I got and came west. Missouri first, then Kansas for a long while. I'm always heading west, it seems."

"And how far west are you headed now?"

"I'm following this river," he said. "To the headwaters, in the mountains near the Continental Divide in Colorado. Men are making a fortune in silver there, and I aim to be one of them."

"Leadville," I said.

"That's right," he said.

"I've heard it is a rough town."

"That's a compliment coming from a resident of Dodge City."

"All I know about it is what I read in the papers."

"They say it snows there on the Fourth of July," he said. "Just imagine, we've been broiling here in the summer heat and, a few hundred miles upstream, it is as cool and fresh as Christmas morning."

"I'd like to see that. Someday."

"What about you, Miss Wylde? May I ask for a bit of your personal history?"

I told him I grew up in Memphis, that my husband had died at the Battle of Spottsylvania Courthouse, and that I had remained unmarried for the past fourteen years.

"You might forgive my mistake, because you wear no wedding band on the fourth finger of your right hand. I am, of course, saddened by your loss. What was his name?"

"Jonathan."

"A good name."

"He was a good man," I said. "But like many good men, he is long dead. I was never one to enjoy the false sympathy prompted by widow's weeds. Not that your expression of sympathy was insincere, of course."

"Of course."

"Also, for professional reasons, you may continue to address me as 'Miss.'"

"Professional reasons?"

"I am a consulting detective," I said. Perhaps I should have added that I was in partnership with Jack Calder, but I did not want to give the impression that I was in some sort of romantic relationship with Calder.

"Whom do you consult?"

"Clients consult me," I said. "In turn, I consult the spirits."

Chatwin laughed.

"I'm not amused," I said.

"Forgive me, but you can't be serious."

"I am quite serious," I said, feeling the blood rush unwillingly to my cheeks. "I am a trance medium and I solve crimes by speaking to the only witnesses who never lie—the dead."

"Sounds like you've rehearsed that."

Of course, I had.

"There is something you could help me with," he said. "I am contemplating testing my luck at the roulette wheel in one of the gambling houses, and perhaps you could give me some numbers to try."

"You confuse me with a fortune-teller."

"Seems like the same line of work," Chatwin said. "No, don't be like that. I truly am interested in the subject. A couple of years ago I read this book by a fellow Englishman, Captain Sir Richard Francis Burton, who talked about extrasensuous perception, the ability to know things beyond the five known senses."

"I am familiar with Sir Richard's books."

"Then surely the dead know all things? Including roulette numbers?"

"The dead know very little, at least those revenants that speak to us."

"Why's that?"

"They haven't crossed over," I said. "They manifest as ghosts here on earth, and they typically have some unresolved business, and they are little aware of anything else. Perhaps the dead who have safely made the passage have greater knowledge, but I have no way of knowing, at least not until my time comes."

"These ghosts," he said. "They have often died gruesome deaths?"

"Some of them."

"Murdered?"

"A few."

"Do they ever name their murderers?"

"In a fashion," I said. "They are generally incapable of answering direct questions, but often the things they say or do, which resemble a sort of

Möbius strip of their turmoil in life, will lead to the perpetrator. At least, that has been my experience with a murdered girl found here in Dodge last year, and other cases since."

"Fascinating," he said.

"Perhaps we can discuss it at length, if your stay in Dodge allows."

"Dash it all," he said. "My train leaves shortly. In a few hours, in fact."

"Not to be, then."

"It seems not," he said. "But who can foretell? On the slim chance that I do not make my fortune in the mountains of Colorado, I may pass this way again, a poorer but wiser man. Would I have your permission to call?"

"Of course," I said. "Our agency is on North Front Street."

"Our?"

"Yes," I said. "I share the business space with a bounty hunter, an individual who is often away in pursuit of some desperado who has jumped bail."

"This bounty hunter," Chatwin asked, his voice suddenly cool. "Is he any good?"

"Yes," I said. "I can tell you from my own experience that Mister Calder is quite good. He is a Texan and has an irritating way about him, but he is expert in the use of persuasive force."

Chatwin smiled.

"Ah, I would expect nothing less," Chatwin said. "Myself, I have foresworn mindless violence. I had my fill of it with the New York gangs and the bloody war."

"But how do you expect to survive in a mining boomtown?"

"I didn't say I wouldn't defend myself."

"Do you mind my asking, what's in the satchel?"

"My lunch," he said. "Apples and cheese. Pipe tobacco and matches. Pencils and a pad for sketching. A book on silver prospecting that remains as closed to me as the Eleusinian mysteries. If only I were a bit smarter, I'm sure I would have an easier time of it."

"You seem full of wit to me."

"Perhaps," he said. "The problem may be that I am inclined to idleness."

"Then you have chosen the wrong profession," I said. "I am told that the life of a miner is filled with toil and danger. Perhaps you would be better suited to gambling, which has its share of danger, but little toil. You mentioned the roulette wheel a moment ago."

"Ah, I tried professional gambling. Three times, as I recall. No head for probabilities, I'm afraid. The roulette wheel is nothing but a hobby these days, and an expensive one at that."

"What do you have a head for?"

"Trouble," he said. "Affairs of the heart, a specialty. Unlucky at cards and all that. Good morning, Miss Wylde."

The thought of saying good-bye to Bruce Chatwin suddenly clouded my mood. I had been lonely for much too long, and he had such a natural conversational style, I longed for more of his company.

"Is there no chance of you remaining in Dodge City," I asked, "even if just a few more hours?"

"Fortune awaits," he said, then grasped my hand. "But we will meet again, I'm sure of it. If not here, then in Leadville, perhaps."

"I doubt it," I said. "I've been in Dodge City for a year now and it looks like I'm here to stay. I always thought I'd resume my journey west someday, but I'm afraid I've grown roots."

"Be careful of making such declarations," he said. "None of us knows what providence has in store for us. We could find ourselves celebrating the Fourth of July with snowflakes frosting our hair."

Then he released my hand and was gone.

7

The door to the newspaper office was standing open, and lying across the threshold was a yellow cat the size of a badger. The cat regarded me with sleepy green eyes, flicked its tail twice, then yawned.

"Pardon me," I said.

Instead of moving, the cat rolled onto its back and exposed its fat stomach.

"I suppose you are expecting to be petted," I said. "But you will be disappointed. I am friends with a very jealous black bird, and he will be unhappy should he discover I've been familiar with a feline."

"Get out the doorway, General Hayes!"

A young man came forward, apologized, and gently shooed the cat away with the side of his foot. The cat flipped over like a spring, spat, and took a swipe at the boy's foot with a forepaw.

"Rutherford B.!"

The cat raced into the street, then sat and regarded the foot and the young man attached to it with contempt.

"You'll be back," the boy said. "When you're hungry."

The boy's name was Walter Shinn and he was the editor of the *Times,* and he had been drinking. He was wearing clothes that looked as if they were in their second or third day of wear, his dark hair was unkempt, and his very blue eyes peered at me from behind a thick set of spectacles that had dark smudges on both lenses.

"Why did you name your cat General Hayes?"

"My brother and I are from Ohio," he said. "I was for General Hayes, but my little brother, Lloyd, was pulling for General Garfield. Now I'm sorry I won the argument."

"You have spots," I said. "On your glasses."

"Oh, thanks." He removed the glasses, breathed on them, and wiped them on the front of his shirt. "Come in, please. Have you heard? Circulation is up to seven hundred fifty now."

"Impressive," I said.

"I'm glad to see you again, Miss Wylde. I wish you would reconsider my offer to picnic with me this Sunday on Gospel Hill. The event would be chaperoned by the church ladies, and I can be a proper gentleman when the occasion requires."

"Why, Walter," I said. "You are just a boy. It would be a scandal. And judging from the state of your clothes, the last proper occasion was some time ago."

"Ah, you break my heart," he said as he led me

back to his desk, which was so cluttered it looked as if every single page of last Saturday's edition had been wadded, creased, and added to the pile. His little brother, Lloyd, was on a stool in front of the type case, his arms folded over a half-finished form, unconscious.

"Is he all right?" I asked.

"He just had too much to drink last night," Walter said. "When he wakes up, he will have a great pain in his head."

"Poor devil," I said.

"Poor printer's devil," Walter said. "All part of the black art." He moved some books and newspapers from a chair beside the desk and asked me to sit. "He will have to learn to hold his whiskey, or he will never a journalist be."

"I should think he could get more done sober."

"Ah, but where's the fun in that?" Walter asked, easing himself into his chair. "Now, what can we do for you, Miss Wylde? Have you been on another ghostly adventure you'd like to share with our readers?"

"I'm afraid not."

"Job printing, then. Excellent. I'll share a secret with you. See that hulking thing in the back?"

"The press?"

"Yes, the Washington hand press," he said. "Journalism is a profitless diversion. It is the job printing generated by the mere possession of the wondrous beast that feeds our cat and keeps us in whiskey. If we eliminated the *Times*, we would have the same money, but twice the leisure in which to spend it."

"But a town needs a newspaper."

"It does drive business to our door," he said.

"And there must be some small satisfaction in seeing your name in print."

"Small," he said. "Some days, small indeed."

"But young as you are—"

"I am twenty-three!"

"—you are an experienced writer, the veteran of thousands of inches of typeset copy. That's why I've come to ask your advice on some literary matters that have been troubling me for some time."

"Literary matters?"

"Yes."

"Not job printing?"

"No," I said.

He opened a drawer of his desk and took out a bottle of whiskey. He uncorked it and poured a few inches into a coffee mug he snatched from the floor.

"Want some?"

"No, thank you," I said.

He shrugged and took a drink.

"I harbor a desire to write," I declared. "Inspired by the Mystery of the Girl Betrayed, and remembering what pleasure I had with books as a young girl, and seeing the interest with which readers snatched up the *Times* account of my adventure, I decided to try my hand."

"And what was the result?"

"Wretchedness itself," I said, surprising myself at the depth of my emotion. "I have defaced many sheets of perfectly good foolscap for no discernible reason. Not only have I failed to bring joy to myself through the effort, but the result is likely to inflict pain on any who bump up against it."

"It can't be that bad."

"But it is," I said. "It is absolute torture."

"Many enjoy the act of composition."

"Fools all," I said. "Graphomaniacs. Hacks and hucksters. Posers and politicians."

He smiled.

"I did not mean you, Walter."

"My fellows on the city council might disagree," he said. "But what you've discovered is the hard truth of the matter, that writing worth reading is hard work."

"I thought you might have, you know, some tricks of the trade."

"Besides whiskey?" he asked. "Well, no. There are none, apart from genius."

"I'm out of luck there."

"Perhaps not," he said gently. "Where I grew up in Ohio, a great emphasis was placed on a classical education, and for a boy of ten or twelve that meant the study of Latin. The word *genius* comes from Latin, and those smart old Romans had a somewhat different concept of the word than we do today. What they meant by it was a kind of guiding spirit that is attached to every individual at birth—and to places and things, for that matter."

"A guiding spirit."

"Yes," Walter said.

"The soul."

"Similar, but not exactly," he said. "We think of giving our souls up to God, but the Romans had enough gods to fill a calendar, with a month left over. So, you had to choose carefully which ones you were going to honor, the ones you thought could do you the most good—or the ones that could do you the most harm if ignored—and you especially had to be mindful of the little gods of the hearth and home, including your own particular genius. And do you know how they honored their personal spirits?"

I shook my head.

"By sacrifice."

"You mean living sacrifices?"

"Animal sacrifices, sometimes," Walter said. "But mostly things that were dear to them: wine, incense, salt. Those things seem kind of cheap in the modern world, but there's one thing that all of us agree is precious."

"Money?"

"Time," he said. "You can recover money, even if you lose a fortune. But you can never get back a single moment of time. And that is what we must sacrifice, if we are to care for our personal genius."

"Time."

"And in ample amounts," he said. "Nothing worth having comes cheap, and we become our own living sacrifices if we are to develop our natural talents. Tell me, Miss Wylde, how long have you been trying to compose your spirit adventures? A few weeks, yes? It will take much, much longer than that. I am twenty-three, as you have already noted, and have been at this trade for nearly five years. I hope to prove competent by the time I am thirty."

"Thirteen years?"

"I am an average study," he said. "For some, it comes quicker."

"Then I will grow old in this apprenticeship."

"We grow old anyway," Walter said.

"Not all of us," I said, suddenly near tears, thinking of poor dead Jonathan. "I'm sorry, I am merely discouraged. This is all more difficult than I thought it might be, and I came here with some silly notion that you could share some kind of recipe with me that would make, well, if not literature, then at least a book-shaped thing. And I discovered that I don't have a writing problem, I have a spiritual problem. Thank you, Walter, for your honesty and wisdom."

"It was the whiskey talking, I'm sure."

"I'm sorry I called you a boy earlier."

"Don't give it a thought."

"You really are very sweet, but my heart belongs to another."

"I know," he said, suddenly sober and sad.

"Have you written that down?" I asked. "I mean, what you just told me."

"No," he said. "Nobody asked me the question before."

"It seems you ought to record it," I suggested.

"I don't think the readers of the *Times* would be amused," he said.

Then the door opened and the cat snarled and a small man dressed in brown plaid with hat in hand stood in the doorway and asked for the proprietor, W. C. Shinn.

8

The man in brown plaid had dark, slicked-back hair and a pencil-thin mustache that danced atop a forced smile, even when he was complaining. The cat, he said, was in need of discipline.

"The feline has drawn blood," the man said, lifting a plaid pants leg to reveal a furrow of bloody welts on his ankle. "Is that your cat, sir?"

"That cat is a citizen of the world," Walter said, giving me a wink. "He darkens whatever door he pleases, helps himself to whatever larder is afforded by generosity or opportunity, and makes a general mockery of the law of ownership."

"I wouldn't know about that," the man in brown said.

"I should think not," Walter said, and held up the whiskey bottle. "Here, pour some of this on that scratch. It is recommended by Dr. Lister."

"I am not acquainted with the man."

"Of course not," Walter said, disappointed. He

returned the bottle to the desk drawer and gave me a look that said he must attend to business.

It was my cue to leave.

"I am grateful for your time," I told Walter, and gave his arm a gentle squeeze. Then I rose and walked toward the door, which was still occupied by the man in brown.

"I am here to place another advertisement," he said. "I am Clement Hill and you may remember me from a few days before, when I placed a notice in your columns. Business has been very good and I believe I will extend my stay—and my notice—for another week."

"Very good," Walter said.

I paused, waiting for Hill to move out of the way, but he lingered.

"If you will excuse me," I said.

"Madam, may I ask you a question?" Hill asked, the mustache bobbing absurdly.

"Anything," I said with wasted sarcasm.

"What is your life worth to you?"

"Excuse me?"

"Your life," he said. "Have you thought about what your life is worth?"

"Constantly."

"Ah, a serious woman," Hill said. "What a delight."

"I could find witnesses who would differ," I said. "But yes, I have pondered the question. So far, there is no answer."

"Ah, I can help," he said. He pulled from his

pocket a narrow pamphlet filled with columns of very small print. "The answer is here."

"I hadn't imagined anyone was keeping track."

"Oh, yes," Hill said. "Now, how old are you? Thirty-five?"

"I'll have you know I am just twenty-nine."

"An honest mistake," Hill said. "Now, here we are. A woman, aged *twenty-nine,* in good health. You are in good health, are you not?"

"I am sound in body if not in mind."

"Not a smoker or a drinker?"

"Smoking is disgusting and I'm somebody else when I drink, so I avoid the hard stuff. I have a glass of wine now and again."

"Quite right," he said, and ran his index finger down the battalion of numbers. "Now, we can assure your life for a thousand dollars for only pennies a day. Pennies."

"Pennies?"

"Thirteen cents a day. Suicide excluded, of course."

"You are selling life insurance."

"Of course."

"The man from the Western Mutual Life Assurance Company, here to protect us from the Deadly Wheel."

"Of course."

"I had some small hope you were engaging me in a conversation about the worth of a human life, instead of a merely pecuniary interest. Tell me, Mister Hill, what is this dreaded wheel? I had an image in my mind of blind and veiled Fortuna spinning her wheel."

"It is the loss of a limb or faculty to mechanization," he said. "We do a good business in policies for brakemen and other railway workers, and for miners, considering the prevalence of accidents in those professions."

"How disappointing that such a poetic phrase is used to describe something so crushingly grim."

The mustache twitched.

"You seem to be an independent woman," Hill said. "A widow, or a grass widow perhaps, and you must have loved little ones who depend upon you. Think of your children's smiling faces, and think what it would mean to them to lose your support. Think of all the hardships that await orphans in this world, and for just a few pennies—"

"Thirteen pennies."

"—a day you can save them the shame of the county poor farm."

"I don't think Ford County has a poor farm. Do we, Walter?"

"Not yet," Walter said. "But there's been talk."

"I don't have children, Mister Hill."

"A sister, then, or a younger brother . . ."

"I am not a gambler," I said. "But if I were, this kind of proposition would strike me as odd. You are asking me to bet against myself, to place a cash wager on the odds of the unthinkable happening. To win the bet, I must die, sooner rather than later, and, of course, I see none of the money—nor do I have anyone to bequeath."

"You are forgetting the funeral expenses," Hill said. "You would not want your brothers and sisters in Christ to bear the cost of your burial without recompense."

"You approach offense."

"How so?"

"You reduce human beings to a column of figures."

"The Western Mutual Life Assurance Company prides itself on the best value for the insurance dollar, madam," Hill said, indignant. "We provide an indispensable service."

"Can you bring people back from the dead?"

"What?"

"If you truly provide the service you say you do, then you would have to bring people back from the dead. Say I'm a little boy who uses my thirteen pennies to buy a policy insuring the life of my mother. If she dies, I don't want the money, I want her back."

"That's absurd."

"Please, Mister Hill," Walter said, stepping forward. "Sit down with me and we can discuss your job printing."

Hill ignored him.

"Take the Sanborn Company," Hill said. "They are a fine company and engaged in a great civic service by mapping, town by town, all of the communities in the West in order to judge their fire risk. They contribute not only to individual security, but they provide a valuable service by encouraging communities to improve their fire battalions."

"Is there a point in sight?" I asked.

"If you have a policy with the good folks at Sanborn—say you are an honest woman with a millinery store, and through no fault of your own that store burns to the ground. You will receive the amount for which you insured your place of business. Nothing could be more fair."

"Nothing could be more cold-blooded," I said. "Perhaps that millinery store—and I'm going to give you the type of business here, although as a woman I'm offended that you didn't say bank or law office—maybe that hat store was the very reason for my existence, perhaps the building had been passed down through generations of women in my family, and perhaps I could see very little point in living once separated from this font of meaning. My point here is the same as with the child, that you cannot restore the mother or the millinery store, you can only settle for farthings."

"That," he said, now wagging his finger at me, "is absurd."

"Remove that finger from my face," I said, "or prepare to lose it."

"Five thousand dollars isn't farthings."

"It's exactly two million farthings, but farthings nonetheless."

I grasped the offending digit and held it fast.

"Unhand me!"

"You infuriate me."

"What have I done?"

"My family had a plantation in Memphis before the war," I said, twisting the finger. "They were slave holders. And the salesmen for the Southern Life Assurance Company of Atlanta came round and sold my father policies on his slaves, so that he would be compensated for the loss of his property should any of them die or be killed. And every few years, he would collect on a policy—five hundred dollars, as I recall, for being deprived through death of the ownership of a human being."

I twistcd the finger a bit more, and Hill shrank with pain.

"And not a penny went to the widows or the orphans."

I released the finger.

"That was all perfectly legal," Hill howled.

"You deserve a thrashing."

"Please," Walter said, stepping between us.

"She is a madwoman," Hill said, vigorously rubbing his finger. "And yet, I find myself strangely attracted to her." Then, to me: "Would you take supper with me at the Dodge House?"

I slapped Clement Hill.

"So, that means no?"

I walked into the street. The cat was sitting on his fat haunches, watching the action through sleepy green eyes.

"Sic him, Rutherford B."

9

My intent was to return to my room at the Dodge House and nap. I was weary and snappish, and an hour or two of sleep might restore my mood and my faculties.

As I passed the Saratoga on my way to my quiet room, I noticed a group of women and children gathered at a wooden table. The women were wearing their Sunday best, even though it was Monday, and the children were leaning forward on their elbows, playing some kind of game. A girl of ten with golden curls spun a teetotum and her eyes sparkled as the wooden top-like thing wobbled and fell.

"Five!" the children squealed, more or less in unison.

The girl moved her token five spaces.

"Cupid," the girl said. "Matrimony is next."

I walked closer, because I knew the game. "The Checkered Game of Life" was common among Union soldiers during the war. The board had sixty-four squares, like a checkerboard, but alternating squares were labeled with all manner of pedestrian boons and calamities, from being rewarded for industry with wealth—and for intemperance with poverty. It was invented by a New York lithographer as a means of teaching moral instruction. I hadn't thought of the game in years, not since Jonathan and I had played before his enlistment.

"You know Mister Bradley's game?" a woman in a blue sun bonnet asked. She cradled a Bible in her arms.

"A version," I said. "But why are you doing this here?"

"As Christian women of the Union Church on Gospel Hill," she said, "we feel a duty to offer wholesome entertainment to those wretches who seek diversion but risk damnation in the pleasure domes of sin around us."

"I'm not sure this is the hour to save the patrons of the Saratoga from themselves," I said. "You might have better luck at ten o'clock at night, rather than ten o'clock in the morning."

"Don't be silly," the woman said. "We couldn't have the children out that late."

"Of course not. What was I thinking?"

"I don't believe we've met," the woman said in a voice choked with forced cheerfulness. "My name is Beatrice Babcock. My husband was Samuel Babcock, but he was called home to Jesus last winter when he was crushed beneath a Murphy wagon full of buffalo hides. The weight of the moisture in those frozen hides snapped the axle and the wagon tipped over."

"I'm sorry."

"Don't be. He is with Jesus. And you are?"

"Not a churchgoer, I'm afraid."

"I didn't mean that, dear. I meant your name. And you are?"

She extended her right hand and I took it.

"Ophelia Wylde."

Her hand wilted in mine.

"Is there something wrong?"

"No," the Widow Babcock said. "I know about you, of course."

"Of course."

"In the *Times.*"

"It wouldn't have been anywhere else."

"I can't say that I approve of what I read."

"Do explain," I urged.

"Editor Shinn reports that you speak to the dead."

"And you find this without credibility."

"On the contrary," she said. "It is because I trust the account that I am disturbed. Leviticus 19 warns us against those who are familiar with spirits, or who are wizards, because we risk being defiled by them."

"Do I look like a wizard?"

"You *are* dressed strangely."

"Let's take a short walk."

"Whatever do you mean?"

"Little pitchers have big ears," I said. "Come with me."

We walked a few yards away.

"And what about what it says in the next chapter?" I asked. "The part about a man or a woman who has familiar spirits or is a wizard shall be stoned to death?"

"Yes, it does say that."

"So you are in favor of stoning?"

"I am a Bible believer, young lady."

"Then you also believe the rest of Chapter 20."

"Absolutely."

"Then let's see what other offenses are punishable by stoning."

I asked to see her Bible.

She reluctantly handed it over.

I found the chapter and ran my finger down the verses.

"Adultery. Death by stoning?"

"Of course."

"A man who lieth with another man."

"Disgusting," she said.

"But death?"

"Sadly, yes."

"How about a beast?"

"It is a chapter on moral instruction," she said.

"And death for the beast as well, it says here. Is that meant for the instruction of other beasts?"

"You are on the verge of blasphemy."

"Which brings us to cursing one's parents."

"What?"

"It's on the list."

"Well, now . . ."

"Says right here that punishment is death by stoning."

"You are twisting my words."

"Here's another: If a man lieth with a woman during her time of bleeding . . . oh, not stoning. Just banishment for them both. Surprisingly lenient, wouldn't you say?"

Widow Babcock snatched the book from my hands.

"That is quite enough," she said.

"As you wish."

"Spiritual darkness," she said. "That is what I am fighting. The town has been cast down into spiritual darkness. I will pray for its deliverance, Ophelia Wylde. And I will pray for you."

I forced a smile.

"How kind," I said. "But I should prefer if you save your prayers for yourself."

Back at the Dodge House, I threw myself on the bed and told myself that I wouldn't sleep, just close my eyes and rest. It was too late in the day to sleep now. In a moment, of course, I was asleep.

10

"When am I going to die?" I ask.

Death smiles.

"We really must bring our visit to a close," he says. "While I have enjoyed our conversation, it has gone on much too long. And I am not going to tell you when your passage is scheduled, not without a directive from the home office."

He looks over at the gold-plated telegraph, which is silent.

"So there you have it."

Death rises from the chair and returns to his paperwork on the other side of the desk. "Go forward and produce your triple naught for the conductor," he says. "You will be promptly disembarked at the next station."

"Triple naught?"

"The temporary pass."

But I don't have the ticket. It's not in either hand and there are no pockets in my dress. I look around the floor at my feet, but there's only the deep purple carpet.

"Did you look in your sleeves?" he says, making a

motion of shoving things into the sleeves of his robe.
"Women often store things there."

I make a snorting noise.

"I'll take your word for it," I say, searching the
wedding dress, which has no pockets and nothing in its
sleeves. "Did you pick this getup out?"

"No, that's always up to the passenger."

"Yeah, right. Not me."

"An unacknowledged desire, perhaps," Death sug-
gests. "But that's not important now. Think of where
you might have dropped the triple naught."

"I must have lost it between cars when we were on
the bridge."

"Did you pause?"

"At first I was terrified," I say. "Then, I wanted to
jump."

"L'appel du vide," Death says. "Call of the void.
The inexplicable urge to jump. Good that you didn't,
because you know what happens when you fall and hit
bottom in dreams. Why didn't you?"

"Why didn't I what?"

"Jump, of course."

"Because Calder pulled me across."

"Calder?"

"My partner, Jack Calder."

"I didn't authorize passage for anyone else," he fumes.
"Where is he now?"

"Don't know," I say. "He hauled me to safety and
then disappeared."

"Highly irregular," Death says. "We must find that
ticket."

"Can you just let me off at the next stop?"

Death shuffles papers on his desk.

"Right?" I ask. "Next stop?"

"You don't understand," Death says.

"You mean if we don't find the ticket, I'm dead?"

"No," Death says. "But you'll be on this train every time you go to sleep from now until the day you die."

11

The knocking on the door came gently, at about 11 o'clock.

"Miss Wylde?" a voice asked.

The knocking had roused me from my dream conversation with Death, and it took me a few moments to realize I was safe in my room at the Dodge House. The knocking continued, which made Eddie bristle his feathers and make a rasping sound deep in his throat.

"Miss Wylde?" the voice came again. "Are you in?"

"Yes," I said. "Yes, I'm here. Who's there?"

"It's Jimmy, the desk clerk."

The damn hotel bill, I thought.

"I know I'm running behind a week," I said. "But I have a new client and I'll bring my account up to date by Friday. Or Monday, at the latest."

"You're a month behind," Jimmy said. "But that's not why I'm here, Miss Wylde. There are some people downstairs asking for you. They said they went to your office and found it closed, so they came here."

I got out of bed and starting dressing.

"Who are they, Jimmy?"

"Doc McCarty and Assistant Marshal Earp."

"Wyatt Earp?" I asked, pulling on my trousers.

"Yes," Jimmy said. "He's back on the police force."

"What do they want, Jimmy?"

"I think you'd better hear it straight from them."

I buckled my belt, then paused. An old fear shot through me.

"Am I in trouble, Jimmy?"

"No, miss," Jimmy said. "It's Charlie Howart. He's done himself in."

McCarty was waiting for me on the bench on the porch of the Dodge House, clutching his Gladstone. He introduced me to Earp, who was leaning against a post with his hands in his pockets, smoking a cigarette and looking out over North Front Street. He was about my age, which is to say about thirty. He was tall, with longish sandy brown hair and a drooping mustache and cold blue eyes. He seemed to swagger even when standing still. McCarty introduced us, and Earp threw his cigarette into the street and disengaged himself from the post with a casual air. He tilted his dark flat-brimmed hat with the back of his hand and nodded in my direction.

"What's this about Charlie Howart?" I asked.

"Hanged himself," Doc said, "or so it appears. His wife, Molly, said she had asked you for help in some odd business Charlie was mixed up in, so we thought you might be able to help."

"I'll do what I can," I said.

"We'll see," Earp said.

It was an odd comment, but I let it pass.

We began walking toward Chestnut Street. The soles of our boots slapped sharply on the hard-packed street, and the air was already warm enough that it seemed to burn my lungs as I took it in.

"Say, Ophie," Doc said. "Are you unwell?"

"Why do you ask?"

"You weren't at your office in the middle of the day, which is uncommon," McCarty said. "We appear to have roused you from bed. And you look as pale as the light of the moon."

"Had some trouble sleeping," I said.

It wasn't a subject I wanted Doc to pursue.

"Read about you in the paper," Earp said.

His voice was low and full of grit.

"I don't know whether to be alarmed or flattered."

"Where's your partner?" Earp asked.

"Calder? He's out chasing a couple of bond jumpers."

"He's a good man in a tight spot," Earp said. "Cool head."

"Sometimes too cool," I said, then continued talking before he could have a chance to ask what I meant. "You were in a recent edition as well, Mister Earp. Your reputation as a peace officer precedes you."

He shook his head.

"Don't be too impressed," he said. "All it takes to be a good cow-town cop is to keep just enough of the peace so the bars stay open and the brothels are full. I've tried my hand at other things—professional gambler, saloon owner, even tried cutting timber for a living up in Deadwood—but failed perfectly at all of them. Hell, I even tried to be an outlaw once, stealing a horse and setting off for Arkansas after they swore out a warrant for my arrest in Lamar, Missouri; but turns out I was equally bad at that. The only thing I can do well is pin a badge on my chest and walk the near edge of catastrophe."

Presently we came to the little house with the two pears out front and the vegetable garden in the back. From the outside, nothing looked amiss, except the front door was standing open.

"Where's Molly?" I asked.

"With a neighbor lady," Earp said.

"Sure you're up to this, Ophie?" Doc asked.

"Of course I am."

"Pardon me," Earp said, "but I'm not clear on what we expect her to contribute. It's not pleasant in that house, and not the sort of scene that should be viewed by a woman. I know she is supposed to be a variety of consulting detective, but it seems clear what happened, so I don't think this is the sort of thing that requires detection. No offense, Miss Wylde."

"None taken," I said. "You are entitled to speak your opinion, Mister Earp, even if your opinion is troglodytic. I would prefer if you address your remarks to me, instead of Doctor McCarty, because I am standing right here and can hear and see you quite clearly."

Doc raised a hand, as if to separate us.

"Let's not get off on the wrong foot here," he said. "Let Ophie take a look. If she doesn't see something we missed, then I'll bet you a beer at the Long Branch."

"Make it a whiskey, and you have a bet."

"I'm glad you gentlemen have found some sport in this," I said.

Taking a deep breath, I slipped through the open door and took a few steps into the parlor, then stopped. The only light was coming in from the doorway behind me, as all of the windows were shuttered tight, and dust motes drifted in the shaft of light. After a minute or two, my eyes adjusted to the gloom.

It seemed that Charlie Howart had hanged himself.

The body was hanging by a hemp rope that had been thrown over a rafter in the center of the room and tied off on one of the legs of the iron stove that squatted near the back wall. The stove was cold on this summer day, of course, but would be a welcome addition during a twenty below Kansas winter.

A knot lay against the right side of Charlie Howart's neck and his head tilted to the left. He was fully dressed, except for his shoes. The toes of his socks hung about a foot from the floor, and an overturned straight chair was nearby.

I closed my eyes and waited in silence for something to come to me. Generally, I can feel the presence of the restless dead, even if there is no apparition. I had expected something—suicides often leave considerable unfinished business behind—but here there was nothing.

I opened my eyes and walked carefully around the body, studying the scene. Something about the rope didn't seem quite right to me, so I stood the chair upright and stepped up on the seat for a better look.

"Find anything in heaven or earth?" Earp asked, a shoulder against the doorway.

"On earth," I said. "Come inspect the rope."

He stepped inside.

"Hard to see anything in here."

"Ask Doc to open the shutters to get some light in."

"Do you really want the neighbors out on the street to see poor Charlie hanging like that?"

"They won't be able to see," I said. "It's so bright outside that the interior will be a featureless void."

"Doc," Earp called. "Open the shutters, will you?"

"Did you ask Molly why they would have the shutters latched?"

"She said they were like that when she found him."

"Charlie must have done it last night," I said. "It must have been for privacy, because there was no wind and certainly no hint of a storm. As hot as it was, one would have all the windows and shutters open. Or, perhaps, somebody else did it to keep curious eyes away."

"Why would you think that?"

"Look at this," I said, pointing to where the rope went over the rafter.

"So?"

"The rope is abraded, for about a yard where it passes over the rafter toward the stove," I said. "The rafter is also grooved beneath the rope, having been worn by the friction of hoisting a heavy weight."

"Charlie was a big man, probably a couple of hundred pounds."

"Yes, but you're missing the point," I said. "Now, if you're going to hang yourself, you throw the rope over the rafter and tie it off, then get up on the chair, put the noose around your neck, and kick the chair away. There's no pressure on the rope when you do it that way, except at the very end. There's not the kind of pressure that abrades the hemp and wears a groove in the rafter."

"So Charlie was hoisted up by somebody else."

"Clearly," I said.

"So, he was murdered."

"We can't conclude that," I said.

"Why not? You just said he didn't do this himself."

"I don't believe he was alive when he was hoisted over the beam," I said. "There are no signs that he fought the rope; all of his fingernails are intact, and there are no scratches around his throat. Did Molly say she heard anything during the night?"

"She didn't mention it."

"There's no gag in his mouth," I said. "If he had been alive, I think he would have been screaming bloody murder. I know I would. He was dead all right when somebody hauled him up, but it might not necessarily have been murder, because he might have killed himself elsewhere, or had an accident, and somebody placed the body here, for effect. Odds are that it was murder, but I don't think we can take it as a given yet."

"Good work, Ophie," Doc said.

Doc had walked inside during my explanation.

"But who would have done this?"

"It would have to be somebody who knew about Howart's fear of a hanged man, because that's what Molly came to talk to me about," I said. "It's asking too much to believe that it was just chance. But Molly told me she didn't tell anyone else."

"That paints Molly with suspicion," Doc said.

"Yes," I said. "But that doesn't feel right."

"Can we cut him down now?" Earp asked.

"Not yet," I said. "I want you to take a look at the knot in this rope."

"The noose?" Doc asked.

"No, the one tied to the leg of the stove," I said. "I'm no expert on these kinds of things, but it looks a bit unusual. There's no real knot there, but it kind of loops around itself and somehow holds fast."

"You're right, Ophie," Doc said, kneeling to examine the knot. "This doesn't look like any kind of cowboy knot I've ever seen. Very unusual."

"Why do an uncommon knot?" Earp asked.

"Well, one uses the knots one knows," Doc said. "Perhaps it's peculiar to a profession, sort of like the surgeon's knot. And, in this case, if you're pulling poor fat Charlie Howart up over the rafter, you probably only have one hand to tie the knot, because the other is busy holding the body up with the other end of the rope. This is the kind of hitch you might be able to do one-handed."

"So that means that it's likely just one person hoisted him up," Earp said.

"That lets out Molly," I said. "She wouldn't have the strength to haul poor Charlie up over the rafter, much less tie the knot with one hand after."

"Good job, Ophie," Doc said, smiling broadly. "Wyatt, I'd like top-shelf whiskey, none of that snakebite remedy they give to the cowboys."

"All right," Earp said grudgingly. "Let's take him down."

"I'd like to sketch the knot first," I said.

"Good idea, Ophie," Doc said.

"Do you have a pencil and paper?"

As Doc reached into his Gladstone and pulled out a small pad and the stub of a pencil, it occurred to me that it might be useful to carry a small bag or satchel with me, a sort of detective's kit that would hold some of the more common things I would need on a case.

I carefully drew the knot, which resembled the number 8 with the letter *G* beneath.

"Got it," I said.

While Earp steadied the body, Doc pulled on the tail of the knot and the rope came free. The lawman caught the body and placed it on the floor as gently as one might tuck a sleeping child into bed.

"Search his pockets," Doc suggested.

While Earp went through the dead man's clothes, I walked slowly around the room. Where was the book that Molly had described? Either stolen by whomever hoisted poor Charlie up over the rafter, or still safely hidden in its secret place. Where would a man hide a book?

The Howart home was little more than a cabin, and sparsely furnished. It consisted of three rooms—the front room, a kitchen, and a bedroom—and I doubted that Howart could have succeeded in hiding the book in either of the latter, because that's where Molly would have spent most of her time. In the front room, there wasn't much between the raftered ceiling and the floor, which had a thin rug thrown over planks of uneven quality. The stove dominated the room, followed by a table with straight-backed chairs and a kerosene lantern on the table. But tucked in one corner was a triangular-shaped bookcase with a door beneath. I went to it and glanced over the few books on the shelves—*Ayer's American Almanac*, some Walter Scott novels, and the family Bible. I opened the door beneath and discovered the cubby hole empty, save for a pile of *Harper's Monthly* magazines. I reached in and felt for the hidden book, but with no luck.

Then I walked around the room, feeling and listening to the boards beneath my feet. None of them was loose or hollow sounding. I looked up at the raftered ceiling, and there seemed no likely spaces to hide a book of any size, at least not where it could be retrieved without the use of a ladder. No, I was looking for an easy, accessible spot.

I looked back at the stove. There was a small space between the bottom of the stove and the bricks it rested on, but when I knelt and peered beneath, it was clearly empty. The stove was cold, so I reached in; my hand felt the bricks to make sure they were all secure. There was firewood in the kitchen, but none beside the stove in the front room, because there had been no need of warmth in many months. There was still a kindling box, however, and it was nearly empty except for a few scrap pieces of wood. The box had been made out of an old peach box and still had the words *GEORGIA PEACHES* burned into the slats on the side. I tilted the box up and shook it, jostling the wood to make sure there was nothing hidden in the bottom, and that's when I noticed an odd muffled sound from the bottom of the box.

I turned the box over and discovered a false bottom that slid away, revealing a space just deep enough to hide a flour sack that held a book-shaped object. I lifted the package and it was as if a jolt of blue flame traveled up my hands and through my arms to pierce my heart. The shock nearly took my breath away.

As I opened the drawstring on the cotton sack, my heart was pounding and my ears were ringing like the new bell on the steeple of the church up on Gospel Hill. I peeked inside and saw a book bound in red Morocco. I pulled the book free of the sack and read the gold lettering, much of which had been worn away, but I could easily read the title from the discolored places where the letters had been:

SYRINX of the SEVEN WORLDS

I turned the book to the spine and there was the name of the author, W. L. Gresham. I opened the book to the title page and the title was repeated, along with a note saying that it was a "metaphysical adventure" and had been published in 1858 in Boston.

"What's a syrinx?" I asked Doc.

I had an image of a syrinx being impossibly old

and possibly Egyptian presiding mysteriously over a desert landscape, like something out of a poem by Percy Bysshe Shelley.

Doc and Earp were still hunched over the body of Charlie Howart.

"Spell it."

I did.

"It's the vocal organ in birds," he said. "It's also the pipes the Great God Pan played. It comes from the Greek, meaning 'tube.' Why?"

I told him.

"Well, there might be something inside."

I opened the book, and a hundred images came to me at once. I pressed the back of my hand to my mouth to keep from uttering a cry. The images were of souls floating in water and souls floating in light and of a great ship that plied ice-strewn waters.

But strongest among the visions was one from the dream where I was in the wilderness in a wedding dress and wading through a trench of blood and bone and steel.

The book was thoroughly, disturbingly haunted.

I snapped the cover shut.

"Come up with anything?" Doc asked.

"I don't think the book has anything to do with birds," I said.

"Well, we found something interesting," Doc said, holding out a railway ticket in my direction. "This was in his vest pocket. It's a round-trip railway ticket to Canon City, Colorado."

12

Wrapped safely in its flour sack, I carried *Syrinx of the Seven Worlds* to the agency. It didn't seem prudent to leave the book at the Howart residence, considering not only was the book dangerously haunted, but whoever had strung poor Charlie up had probably been looking for it.

I took the book out of its sack and placed it carefully on my desk, drew the shade, and lit the lamp. Then I took a deep breath and opened the book. As before, my hand tingled with something otherworldly. First, I went to the last page—it was 307, just as in my dream—then flipped back to the front matter.

When I released the book, I found that the haunting sensations stopped. While touching the book was disturbing, reading it was not. In fact, the reading of the book seemed absolutely neutral. I noted the fact, and returned my attention to the title page.

In addition to the information about the date and place of publication, there was a faded stamp across the bottom of the page: *Property of The Denver City and Auraria Reading Room and Library Association.* A handwritten note on a slip of paper nestled beside the title page indicated the book was due back April 22, 1860.

The book was overdue by more than 18 years.

I turned the page and scanned the Table of Contents, which listed the titles of the book's seven parts, in this manner:

> *Chapter the First: Darkness. Being a meditation on the void between worlds; the appearance of our adventurer and his passage on a comet; his arrival on antique shores; his confusion regarding this mortal coil; and his eventual discovery of the hidden and narrow passages between worlds.*

I will summarize the other chapters.

> *Chapter Two: Water (ancient Mars).*
> *Chapter Three: Light (the sphere of love).*
> *Chapter Four: Life (the chains of Earth).*
> *Chapter Five: Death (the domain of Saturn).*
> *Chapter Six: Dreams (the Mountains of the Moon).*
> *Chapter Seven: Rebirth (the symphony of Venus).*

Each chapter was long, and tracked the progress of this unnamed pilgrim from world to world.

It was the kind of story I would normally find
intriguing, but the writing was baroque, cryptic,
and old-fashioned; it was about as enjoyable as
reading a multiplication table but made much
less sense. I skipped to the chapter on dreams,
thinking I might find some clue to my own sleeping drama, but it was more of the same impene-
trable prose. The author, Gresham, was either a
genius who was speaking on a plane that was far
beyond my comprehension, or he was a lunatic.

Why would this book figure so heavily in my
dreams, when I had no obvious connection to
the story? The book must be important, to figure
so in my dreams, to be kept hidden by Charlie
Howart, and to be as haunted as it was.

My only recourse was to ask W. L. Gresham
himself.

I paged back to the front, looking for the address of the publisher.

OLD STATEHOUSE PUBLISHING CO.,
924 CONSTITUTION AVE.,
BOSTON, MASS.

I got out a fresh sheet of paper, loaded my
pen from the inkwell, and composed a letter to
Gresham, in care of the publisher.

13

Molly Howart sat in the chair she'd sat in only two days before. She was clutching Western Mutual Life Assurance Company Policy No. 784 in her lap, pleading with eyes that were even more sorrowful than before.

"They are denying the claim," she said. "Mister Hill says that Charlie's death was a suicide. Do you believe he took his own life, Miss Wylde?"

"I don't know, Molly," I said.

"Not for a minute do I think he committed suicide," she declared. "Not Charlie. I don't understand what secret he was guarding, but I know he wouldn't have chosen that way out."

"May I get you some tea?" I asked. I'd read somewhere that when confronted with someone in distress, the thing to do was to offer tea.

"It's bad enough that Charlie is dead," she said. "But now I am faced with a penniless widowhood."

"I think a cup of tea might be the thing."

"There is no one I can turn to," she said. "My family in Missouri is dead, all of them, and without Charlie I am a woman alone. I will be able to survive well enough for the rest of the summer, but winter will come. Then what will I do, with all of the food gone and no money?"

"No tea, then."

"What did you determine from the book?"

"Very little, I'm afraid," I said. "The book is quite haunted, but remains a mystery. Whatever connection it may have to the case remains unclear."

"Did you find nothing that might exonerate my Charlie?"

I told her how the rope showed signs of having borne weight after it was thrown over the rafter, but I said that the detail in itself was probably insufficient to challenge the insurance company.

"Doctor McCarty is delaying any official determination of the cause of death," I said. "As county coroner, he needs more evidence to make a ruling. But I'm afraid he's about exhausted his sources of inquiry."

Molly looked at her hands, flightless birds in her lap.

My heart slid toward my stomach.

There would be no money from this case, even if I could prove that Charlie Howart did not commit self-slaughter, for how could I take even a dime of a poor widow's insurance money? Even if she had the means to pay my twenty dollars a week plus expenses—and it might take many days indeed—there was no guarantee I could bring her satisfaction.

There were expenses of my own I had to pay, of course. My half of the rent on the agency here on North Front Street, and my weekly bill for my room at the Dodge House, and my meals and Eddy's seed, and the chair I sat in, and the paper I had written the publishing company on. Being a consulting detective wasn't a hobby, as Calder kept reminding me, but a trade. You wouldn't go to Zimmerman's hardware down the street and expect him to give you a new Martini and Henry buffalo rifle just because he likes dealing in guns, would you? (Actually, I had no idea if Zimmerman dealt in such rifles, or if the Martini and Henry company made buffalo rifles, but being ignorant of firearms, it was the only type and make of gun I could summon from memory to use as an example.) My point—and here I had to admit I was arguing with myself—was that I deserved to be paid. Why, Doc McCarty wouldn't treat anyone without asking for—

And that's where my argument crumbled, because I knew Doc treated everyone, whether they could pay or not. Oh, he would take their money if they could afford it (and he supplemented his income with the drug store next door), but if they couldn't, he treated them anyway and didn't make them feel as if they were somehow inferior human beings. What Doc looked at first was need, and in an emergency, there was no time to be pulling out the ledger books.

"*Merde,*" I exclaimed.

There had to be a better way to make a living at being a consulting detective, but thinking like that was pulling the ledger book out first. I could figure that out after I helped my client.

"I beg your pardon?" Molly asked.

"I'm sorry," I said. "I was just thinking out loud."

"Did you have an idea?"

"Perhaps," I said.

I retrieved the ticket that Doc had taken from Charlie Howart's body and slid it across to her.

"What do you make of this?"

"The railway ticket? I told Doctor McCarty I had no idea why Charlie would have a ticket for Canon City. He never had any business there, as far as I know of."

"Might I make use of it?"

"Use it how?"

"To go to Canon City and make some in-quiries," I said. "It's a round-trip ticket, on the Santa Fe with a transfer to the Denver & Rio Grande, and it has some cash value to you. But it might be worth more to pay my passage to Canon City and back. It's the location of the state prison—which was the territorial prison until just two years ago—and perhaps Charlie's business had something to do with someone incarcerated there."

"Then you'll help me?"

"I can't promise results," I said. "But I can promise I will do my best."

"Do you want my twenty dollars now?"

"No, Mrs. Howart. Keep your money."

Molly started to cry.

"Please, don't."

She pulled a kerchief from her sleeve and dabbed her eyes.

"I can't help it," she said.

"Doesn't some tea sound good right now?"

She shook her head.

There was a knock at the agency door. Through the window, I could see Wyatt Earp slouching in the door frame, a cigarette smoldering beneath his mustache.

I asked Molly to excuse me.

"I'm sorry, Marshal Earp," I said, after opening the door a crack. "As you might notice, I am quite occupied with a client. Perhaps you could come back at a more convenient time."

"Sorry, Ophie."

"Only my closest friends are allowed to call me Ophie," I said. "We may never reach that level of familiarity, so I suggest you not become too fond of using the diminutive of my name."

"I have no idea what you just said."

"Just call me Miss Wylde."

Earp nodded, and removed his hat.

"Miss Wylde," he said. "I'm sorry to intrude, but I have paper for you."

"Paper? I don't understand."

"Paper," he said. "An official document."

"A warrant?"

"Something like that."

"For my arrest?"

"Actually a subpoena," he said. "You are hereby compelled to appear at Federal District Court at Denver in the matter of the people versus Eureka Smith."

He handed me a tri-folded sheet of paper with my name on the outside.

"The spirit photographer case?"

"Don't know anything about it," Earp said. "My job is just to serve the paper."

"When?" I asked.

"It's right there," he said, pointing to the paper. "Ten in the morning, Thursday, June 27."

"That's two days away. What if I can't make it?"

"That's a subpoena," Earp said. "It's a command from the court to appear."

"But that's Colorado," I protested. "Surely a court in Colorado can't force me to appear."

"It's a federal court," Earp said. "State lines don't matter."

"What if I can't afford the travel?"

"You'll have to take that up with the court—in person."

"This is outrageous."

"Outrageous or not, you must appear."

"What if I don't?"

"You would be held in contempt of court. You could be fined, or they could send somebody like me to arrest you."

"Fils de salope," I muttered.

"It is enough to make one cuss," Earp said. "Good day, Miss Wylde."

14

"I have a ticket," I say.

Death reached across the desk and took the pass from my hand. He gave it a quick examination with his expressionless black eyes and promptly returned it.

"How unfortunate for you," Death says. "This is a ticket to Colorado, something you've carried over from your waking life."

"All I can read are numbers," I say. "The letters are a jumble to me."

"It is of no use to you here," he says. "Our line doesn't make the run to Canon City, at least not yet."

I frown.

"That was a joke," he says.

"Death isn't funny."

"So I've been told," he says.

"What can you tell me about a book by a lunatic named Gresham," I say.

"More questions. Truly?"

He would have raised his eyebrows if he'd had any.

"The book is titled . . ."

"I know the title of the book," Death says. "But this is not a question that I am allowed to answer."

"So there is some connection."

"It would violate home office rules for me to tell you whether there was a connection or not," Death says. "This is something that you must work out for yourself, for only you can decide if there is a connection."

"So, if I asked you what the meaning of life is . . ."

"The answer would be the same. You must work it out for yourself, while entertaining the possibility that there is no meaning at all."

"That would suggest that the only real meaning is in the rigor you bring to the question. Many people would be tempted to say that life is what you make it, or that you make your own meaning, but that's too easy. You could come up with something silly like saying puppies and sunsets are the meaning of life."

Death stares impassively at me.

"You think I could have a few minutes to talk directly with Charlie Howart back there in the baggage car? If you would be kind enough to call your widdershins away from his coffin for just a few minutes so I could have a word, it might prove terribly useful to the case I'm working on up there, in my waking life."

Death folds his robed arms.

"Go look for the temporary pass," he says. "If you don't find it, you will be trapped on this train forever in your dreams. There's only one way out, and that's to step off at the end of the line—in which case your

waking life ceases as well. The other option is to stay aboard and eventually go mad. And I'm not sure but that I wouldn't go mad as well for having to suffer your questions."

15

I moved out of the Dodge House before dawn on Wednesday morning, the day after receiving the subpoena, but left a note promising to pay my outstanding balance within the month—even though I didn't know how I was going to manage it. It scared me to be moving out of the hotel, because the room was pleasant and clean, and had been the only safe place I'd known since my childhood. But better to move out, I thought, than be thrown out.

It took me only a few trips to walk my belongings to the agency, where Eddie already awaited me in his cage. There was neither a bed in the office nor a washstand, but I would have to deal with those everyday things once I returned from Colorado.

It was 400 miles to Denver.

I had gone to the Dodge City depot and traded the round-trip ticket to Canon City for a one-way ticket to Denver, and had gotten one dollar and fifteen cents in change.

By rail, it would take only 27 hours, counting the time for stops and to change trains. Starting at the Santa Fe depot at Dodge, I would head west for 275 miles. At Pueblo—in the middle of the night—I would board a northbound Denver & Rio Grande train for the rest of the way, arriving in Denver at nine o'clock in the morning. I hoped that would give me enough time to walk to the courthouse.

At ten minutes before time for me to board the train, I sat at my desk in the agency, my valise packed, and a letter to Doc McCarty in front of me. The letter explained my trip to Denver and asked that Doc—who had a key to the agency—would visit Eddie twice a day, to feed and water and talk to him. I had considered writing a letter to Calder as well, but I didn't know when he would be back—or if he would care when he was.

"Dammit, Jack," I said.

Eddie beat his wings, as he knew something was amiss.

"Nevermore!" he cried. Then, uncharacteristically, he slipped into another poem. *"Dream within a dream!"*

He had been taught to utter the lines for a stage act in which I recited bits and pieces of Edgar Allan Poe, and he finished many of the lines for me. The act was part of a larger spook show in which I would cheat people out of their money by pretending to answer, from the spirit world, their questions about dead loved ones. We hadn't performed the act in more than a year.

"I'm sorry, Eddie," I said. "Perhaps we can play the game, just you and me, when I get this rotten Colorado business finished."

He stretched his wings and cocked his head and gave me a look that signaled incredulity.

Then it was time to go.

I started for the door, then hesitated. Going back to my desk, I removed *Syrinx of the Seven Worlds* and slipped it into my bag. Then I closed and locked the door behind me.

Pausing next door, I knelt to slip the note to Doc McCarty under the door to the pharmacy.

"Miss Wylde," someone called behind me. "Oh, Miss Wylde."

It was Rose, from the China Doll, clutching her butterfly-pattern silk robe flapping loosely around her.

"He's gone," she said. "The Sky Pilot is gone."

"I'm sorry, Rose," I said, standing up. "Was he better?"

"Much better, but Miss Phossy say he no longer can stay in the storeroom without doing work. When I go to check on him this morning, he was gone. What do I do?"

"I don't think there's anything you can do, Rose."

"But what if he walks off onto the prairie again?"

"It's not like you could have kept him chained up," I said.

"Yes," she said, misunderstanding. "I should have used a chain to keep him from getting away."

"No," I said. "He may be crazy, but he's a grown man, and you have to let him make his own decisions—even if it is to walk into prairies in the middle of a Kansas summer."

"I don't understand him," Rose said. "He had everything here. A place to stay, plenty to eat. And he had me. He had me, Miss Wylde, as a friend. All he had to do to make Miss Phossy Jaw happy was to do a little sweeping and cleaning. He decided to walk away instead."

"Men," I said. "They'll break your heart every time."

"Oh, Miss Wylde," Rose said. "My heart's been broken so many times it's just like the china doll of the name, you know? Thrown down and cracked and not in one piece anymore. But I just wanted to be his friend."

I embraced Rose, patting her gently on the shoulder.

"You go drink some tea. You'll feel better."

She stared at me.

"I have to catch a train, Rose," I said. "But I hope you find your Sky Pilot. None of us has enough friends that we can afford to lose one."

"I just hope he's still alive," Rose said.

Then I picked up my valise and walked to the depot, where the hulking and huffing black locomotive and yellow cars were waiting. The sky was the color of gunmetal, and the temperature was already uncomfortably hot; in another few hours, it would be another Kansas scorcher.

As I stepped from the platform to the train, I remembered the last time I had boarded a train with almost no money in my pockets and facing an uncertain future—that had been just over a year ago, when I boarded the train that brought me to Dodge City.

16

"Do you swear to tell the truth, the whole truth, and nothing but the truth?"

Sitting in the witness stand, with my hand on the Bible, and before a packed federal courtroom, I swore that *so help me God* I would. The crowd didn't make me nervous—I had played to audiences this large or larger—but my appearance did worry me. I hadn't slept on the train, my clothes were covered in the dust and cinders that accompany steam travel, and my hair—well, let's just say my hair had notions of its own.

"Would you state your name and your current address?" the prosecuting attorney asked. He was an imposing, white-headed figure who had a habit of planting his feet and addressing his remarks to the ceiling over the jury box.

"Ophelia Wylde," I said. "Dodge City, Kansas."

"What is your occupation, Mrs. Wylde?"

"I prefer Miss Wylde," I said. "For the past year, I've run a consulting detective agency."

"Is there anything unusual about this agency?"

"I don't think so."

"I'd advise you not to play games with the state." This was directed in a booming voice to a spot about six feet above my head. "Answer the question, please."

It was at this point that I noticed, over to the side of the courtroom in the first row, a disreputably dressed group of men chomping on cigars and pipes, and with notebooks and pencils at various states of ready. Reporters. Every Denver paper appeared to be represented, as well as an out-of-town correspondent or two.

"Miss Wylde."

"I answered your question," I said. "I don't think there's anything unusual in what I do. And I've traveled four hundred miles in the past twenty-seven hours to appear here, for a reason I know not, at considerable expense and tribulation, not to mention the toll it has taken on my personal appearance. I must look like a banshee."

Laughter rippled through the courtroom.

The judge rapped his gavel.

"The jury is instructed to carefully separate the travel-worn appearance of the witness from the credibility of her statements," he said. He was a gentle man, with longish black hair and a pair of spectacles perched on the bridge of his nose.

"Does that include her mannish dress?" the prosecutor asked.

"Mister Smith, this is ordinarily the place where

your attorney would object to such a remark," the judge said, directing his remarks to a pale and small-looking man hunched at the defense. "I am pointing this out as an example of the burden you have placed upon yourself by being your own counsel."

"I can afford no lawyer," Smith said.

"Very well," the judge said. "The jury is advised that a manner of dress is little indication of veracity, and that Miss Wylde's attire—while unusual—is appropriate for the setting. This is still the west, and only a little removed from the frontier, and we cannot expect professional women to dress as do the ladies in Boston or New York."

"Understood, your honor."

"Miss Wylde," the judge continued, "you suggest that you don't understand why you've been called as an expert witness here. Is that the case?"

"It is, sir. I rushed here from the train depot and just arrived in the courtroom in time to hear my name called. I have conferred with no one about my reason for being here."

"The court apologizes," the judge said. "But that was the intent. You have spoken to no one regarding your appearance here today?"

"Only the unpleasant man who served the papers to bring me here," I said, "and he was remarkably uninformed about the affair."

"And you do not personally know anyone here in the courtroom today?"

"No, they are all strangers to me."

"As are the clients of Eureka Smith?"

"I have met none that I am aware of."

The judge nodded.

"This is an unusual feature in an unusual case," the judge continued. "The court has called upon you as an expert witness because of the particulars of the charges. My name is Judge Isaac Stone. Mister Eureka Smith, the man sitting at the table there, has been accused of fraud for producing photographs that purport to show departed loved ones. The prosecution feels that this is part of a scheme to extort money from bereaved families here in Denver. Mister Smith has pleaded not guilty to the charges and claims the images have actually captured the shades of these beloved individuals. Would both you, Mister Smith, and you, Mister Decker, agree that this accurately summarizes the problem before the court?"

"I do," the prosecutor boomed.

Smith nodded.

"Please stand when you address the court," the judge said. "And you must speak, so that your words can be captured by the court reporter."

Smith stood, somewhat unsteadily. His brown suit, which was much too big, was of a fashion that went out before the Civil War.

"Yes, your honor," Smith said.

"Good," the judge said. Then he turned to me. "What the court would like is for you to attempt an experiment for us."

"What kind of experiment?" I asked. "Your honor, I mean."

"We want you to examine some photographs that Mister Smith has taken and render an opinion as to whether they are genuine or not."

"Sir, I am unfamiliar with the photographic process."

"There is another expert, an Abraham Bogardus, who will inform the jury about the scientific principles involved. What we would like you to do is to examine the photographs and tell us whether you think, well, whether you believe they capture actual ghosts."

"All right," I said. "I can try."

"That's all we can ask," the judge said.

"But how on earth did you decide on me?"

"Let's try to keep our questions to a minimum," Judge Stone said. "Suffice it to say the court has read about your exploits in some of the western papers and noted your claimed expertise in otherworldly communication."

I nodded.

"What will happen now is that both sides get to question you about your credentials, which includes your education and background and so forth. Mister Decker, proceed."

The prosecutor thanked the judge, then stood and approached me.

"Let's see, I believe my last question was about your current occupation."

"Yes," I said. "I'm a consulting detective."

"And I asked if there was anything unusual about your work. Now, I'm going to ask that question again, but a bit differently—would an ordinary person consider there is anything unusual about your work?"

"Well, as the judge said, it involves communication with the dead."

"So, you talk to spirits."

"Yes, sir. Or rather, they talk and I listen."

"How do they talk? Is it like you and I speaking now?"

"Not like that," I said. "Seldom are there direct questions or answers. It's more like I get to listen as they talk to themselves, or sometimes they act out things that happened in life that aids the detection of crime."

"What kinds of crime?"

"All kinds," I said. "But murder a specialty."

"Murder, is it?" he asked.

"It's printed on our cards."

"Our cards?"

"My partner is a bail bondsman and bounty hunter."

"I see. And how long have you been doing this?"

"A year now."

"And how were you occupied before that?"

"I didn't have a regular job," I said quietly.

"Were you a wife and mother, then? Or a school teacher?"

"No," I said.

"Speak up, please. The jury cannot hear you."

"No," I said louder.

"Tell us, then, precisely what you were."

I remained silent.

"Are we to guess?" Stone asked. "Should we start our list with fallen woman and—"

"No," I said. "Nothing like that."

"And yet you do not enlighten us."

Decker put his hands in his vest pockets and turned away from me.

"Miss Wylde," the judge said. "You must answer the question."

"I was a trance medium."

"I'm sorry, I'm not sure I understand."

"A trance medium," I said. "But I was a fake. I did exactly what Eureka Smith is accused of doing now, only I didn't use photographs. But it was trickery just the same. I pretended to contact the dead in order to extract money from my clients."

"Isn't that what you do now?" Decker asked.

"No," I said. "I discovered—well, quite accidentally I discovered that I actually could speak to the dead. I confirmed that the tenets of Spiritualism, which I had believed in when young, were true, that the spirit does survive the death of the physical body. And I learned that I could help these restless ghosts cross over."

"Cross over?"

"To leave their attachment to the earth and continue their journey."

"To heaven?"

"You could think of it that way."

"How about hell?"

"None of the spirits I've helped seemed bound for that place," I said. "Which is more than I can say for some of the living persons I meet every day."

More laughter, and more gavel rapping.

"And you charge for this service?" Decker asked.

"Not really," I said. "Oh, I mean to, but I can't bring myself to take any money from the people we help. I feel too guilty."

"You won't be in business long."

"That's what my partner says."

Stronger laughter. Harder gavel banging.

Decker walked over and placed a hand on the witness box, as if he were about to counsel an errant daughter. He looked me in the eye now, for the first time.

"Let me be sure we have this right," he said. "You were once a liar and a cheat, but aren't anymore. You really can talk to ghosts, but you can't get all of your questions answered because they don't converse like us. You solve crimes with the aid of these spirits, but you don't charge the people who are helped by these acts of supernatural detection because you feel guilty. Is that about right?"

"It sounds bad when you put it like that."

"I wouldn't know any other way to put it," Decker said, then looked away. "You must admit that it sounds quite damning. Can you not admit that?"

"No," I said. "You take—"

"That's all," Decker said. "I have no more questions."

"But I didn't get to finish," I protested.

"There was no question left unanswered," he said.

"Pardon, Mister Decker, but there was," the judge said. "You asked Miss Wylde to admit that it sounded damning and you did not let her finish."

"It was rhetorical, your honor."

"From where I sit, there is no such thing," the judge said. "Miss Wylde, you may finish your answer."

I nodded my thanks.

"You might compare my habits to that of a great many citizens of Denver City on a Sunday morning. They sit in a church pew and sing praises to a being that can neither be seen nor heard. They listen with their hearts, and many of them believe they have direct communication with this otherworldly presence. They are earnest in these endeavors, or at least most of them are. They have no promise of material gain. Their only recompense lies in the spiritual realm. They are told that the sins of the past have been forgiven. Never once are they accused of charlatanism or trickery or dissembling."

There was silence in the courtroom.

"Nothing more, your honor," Decker said.

"Mister Smith," the judge said, "it is now your opportunity to ask questions."

Smith stood stiffly.

"Thank you, but no," he said. "I have no questions."

"None at all?" the judge asked.

"No, sir. I will let my work speak for itself."

The defendant sat down.

"Very well," the judge said. "Thank you, Miss Wylde. You may step down, but please remain close at hand. The court will now take a thirty-minute recess, in which opposing counsel will meet in camera to discuss particulars of the experiment."

The gavel came down so hard it made my ears ring.

17

Abraham Bogardus had a broad white beard that touched his chest, but his eyes were young and sharp. He had been appointed to explain to the jury—twelve men who smoked and chewed and sat sleepily with their thumbs hooked in the armholes of their vests—the technical aspects of photography, as a primer to the experiment that would soon commence.

In a clear voice, honed from years of lecture, he gave his biography. He had learned the art and science of the daguerreotype in 1846, just seven years after Professor Louis Daguerre had given his invention to the world. Bogardus had opened a gallery in New Jersey and soon found such success that he relocated to Broadway in New York, and since that time has been regarded as one of the giants of photography, or at least that's what he told the jury. American photography, he added, was superior in every way to the old European kind, because of the Yankee passion for experimentation. He currently resided in Philadelphia, where he had a celebrated studio and gallery.

Decker asked if he ever had been asked to investigate claims of the supernatural.

In 1869, Bogardus said, he had been a witness at the trial of spirit photographer William H. Mumler, whose most famous image was that of Mary Todd Lincoln, with the assassinated president hovering behind her chair, reaching out with ghostly hands to comfort his widow.

"What did you conclude about this portrait?" Decker, the prosecutor, asked.

"I concluded that it was the product of trickery," Bogardus said.

"What means did you use to reach this conclusion?"

"Upon examination, it was apparent to me that the image was made through use of a common double exposure, either by accident or by design. Because of the care taken in the composition of the photo of Mrs. Lincoln, I would guess the latter."

"A double exposure," Decker said. "Could you explain?"

"Yes, either by re-exposing the wet plate, while it is still in the camera, with a different scene, or by using a plate that already has an existing image on it, but which has not yet been fixed. This latter has happened to me quite often in my career. Photographers often reuse plates, because a simple mistake in preparation or development can ruin an image; the plates must be prepared and processed in an orange tent, for example, to allow the photographer to see his work, because the plates are sensitive to blue light only. Sometimes, a plate is reused simply because the image is not pleasing. If the plate is not buffed and cleaned thoroughly before its reuse, then a ghostly image will remain."

"And this is known to many photographers?"

"All, I would dare to say," Bogardus said, his beard wagging. "It was known from very nearly the beginning of the science that effects could be achieved through photography that appeared to represent otherworldly things, but it is a trick of reducing several moments in time to a single image. The earliest instance I can recall is the treatise on stereoscopy by Sir David Brewster in 1856. As an afterthought, Sir David describes the ghostly forms that result when someone walks unintentionally in front of the camera during an exposure. While all other nonmoving objects in the frame are distinct, the moving person appears wraith-like. It is uncanny, but perfectly in the realm of the rational."

"Tell us how large these plates are," Decker prompted.

"A full daguerreotype plate is six and one half by eight and one half inches, and all plate sizes—whether copper, glass, or tin—are based on this original size, from half plates right on down to sixteenth plates, which are too small in my opinion to be of much value, but which have become ubiquitous."

"And Mumler used a full plate?"

"It varied. Most were *cartes-de-visites,* about the size of a playing card."

"What about our defendant, Eureka Smith?"

"That is the only point on which Mister Smith and I would agree," Bogardus said. "He uses a full wet plate, a glass plate. A collodion. The full plate glass negative is a superior process and has the virtue of being able to produce an unlimited number of exact photographic prints on albumen paper."

"As to the Mumler photo," Decker said, "you concluded it was fakery from inspection alone?"

"Oh, no," Bogardus said. "I produced a very fine spirit photo myself, to prove the ease with which it could be done. My subject was Phineas T. Barnum, and I made a double-exposure image that showed Abraham Lincoln hovering over his right shoulder."

"P. T. Barnum?" Decker asked.

"Oh, yes," Bogardus said. "He was keen to expose spirit photography as humbuggery and pressed the case against Mumler. Although Barnum is a master of humbug himself, he says he never exploited grieving family members for money, just natural human curiosity, and that he always gave full value."

"Thank you," Decker said, then smiled at the jury. "Your witness, sir."

Smith stood and walked slowly toward Bogardus, but kept his eyes down.

"Not everyone believed Mumler was a faker."

"You'll have to speak up," the judge said.

"Not everyone believed that William Mumler was perpetrating a hoax, did they?"

"No," Bogardus said. "He fooled a lot of people."

"And one of those people was a journalist, Moses Dow?"

"Yes."

"Dow commissioned a sitting, and monitored the process, and reported the result as a spirit photograph of himself with a recently departed acquaintance, a young woman, standing behind him."

"There is no question there, sir," the judge said.

"Wasn't that his testimony?"

"Dow was a spiritualist and had no training in the science of photography."

"What was the result of the trial?"

"I object," Decker said, jumping to his feet.

"You have opened the door by your extensive questioning of Professor Bogardus on the subject of the Mumler case," the judge said. "I must allow it."

"What was the verdict?" Smith asked.

"Mumler was acquitted," Bogardus said.

Smith walked back to his seat, and the judge excused the professor from the witness stand.

"Now comes something a bit out of the ordinary," the judge said, addressing the jury. "Miss Ophelia Wylde, who you heard from earlier as to her unique credentials as a witness in this case, has agreed to submit to an experiment to help us determine the truth. She will be placed in the jury room behind us with five photographs to examine, and asked to determine if any of them represent a true spirit image. She has seen none of the photographs before, and has had no contact with either the living subjects in the photos or the persons—including Mister Eureka Smith— who made them. After she is seated with the photographs, the room will be sealed, and no communication will be permitted until the time she has reached a decision, or has failed to do so, and will indicate this by rapping three times upon the door. The jury will then hear her conclusions."

18

The bailiff escorted me into the jury room with the same stern face I imagined he reserved for murderers, then closed the door behind me. The sound of his key in the lock as the room was secured sent a chill down my back, and I couldn't help but feel that I was on trial.

I was hungry and tired and suffering from lack of sleep, but there was nothing to do but proceed. If I had declined to accept the challenge, the pack of reporters outside would have pilloried me.

The room was long and narrow, with a walnut table down the center, and on the table were five photographs. There were no chairs. The room had windows along one side, but each had been sealed with black cloth and tape. The only light in the room came from a tri-burner gas lamp planted in the center of the table, fed by a narrow copper tube that came from the ceiling. The

flames burned brightly in their globes, spilling
three circles of light over the five photographs.

Each photograph was printed from a full plate,
on albumen paper, and in tone and quality they
seemed alike. Each purported to show a living
sitter with a ghost hovering nearby; three of the
sitters were men and two were women; and the
only identification on the photos were the labels
A through *E*.

I walked down the length of the table, pausing at each photo.

A was of a young man with flowing dark hair
and a handlebar moustache clutching a wooden
cross to his chest, which gave the impression that
he was a preacher or had some other religious
affiliation. He was angled to his right in the chair
and looking earnestly down at the cross, giving
the impression he was lost in thought or prayer.
Behind him was an old man in white, staring
straight into the camera, with a look that suggested reproach. The old man's features were so
similar to that of the sitter that one naturally
began forming a story, that the young man had
somehow lost the path and that the dead father
watched in disapproval from beyond.

I reached down and touched my forefinger to
the photo.

"Fake," I said.

Not only was it just too perfectly composed,
with all of the elements needed to suggest a story
to the viewer, but I felt nothing when I touched
the paper.

I moved on to the next.

B also had a man as the sitter, an older gentleman with pork-chop whiskers and a pudgy face. He also was looking to his right. Behind him there was an indistinct pale figure that looked as if it might be a child—or an orangutan. A cartoonish arm was draped around the left shoulder of the man, holding an equally cartoonish flower beneath his nose. A dead daughter, perhaps? A beloved ape? Whatever the intent, the result was laughable.

I placed my finger on the photo, and felt nothing.

"Next," I said.

Photograph *C* was of a young woman, seated, but staring emotionless at the camera. She was dressed in widow's weeds. Behind her was a pale (the ghosts in this collection were universally pale) figure, clearly wearing an officer's uniform, that of a Union captain. He seemed to float crazily over the woman's right shoulder. The story was clear enough, and I wanted to avoid thinking about it, so I moved on.

Photograph *D* was of the third man. The sitter was perhaps forty years old, facing his right, as with the others. His most remarkable feature was his head of black hair, as straight and as coarse as a paintbrush, which he parted on the side. He had no facial hair. His left hand was holding a book to his chest in a casual way that did not suggest it was a Bible. His right hand held a cigar with an expensive-looking band. He was dressed in rich and contemporary clothes, and he gazed into the distance with a sly smile.

Behind him appeared a sorrowful ghost.

I leaned down to get a closer look.

This figure was lighter than the other apparitions—being a shade of smoke gray instead of cloud white—but had detail the others lacked. For one, he was bound in chains. For another, his face was frozen in some kind of agony. The chains crossed his chest and went up to each of his upraised hands, which appeared bound to the wall behind him. So contorted were his features that it was impossible to determine his age, but there was the indication of a short beard. The other remarkable feature was that there seemed to be a pickaxe leaning against the wall next to him.

What was the story?

I couldn't guess.

The technique was so good, and the appearance of the sorrowful ghost so powerful, that I would have guessed that this was a product of the learned fakery of Professor Bogardus. But if that were the case, wouldn't he have made something that invited the viewer to weave a story? It just didn't make sense, pairing a well-dressed man of our time with something that looked like it belonged in a tale from the Brothers Grimm.

I did not touch the photograph, not yet.

The fifth photograph, *E*, was of a dour old woman in a dark cap and dress squarely facing the camera. Behind her was the obligatory pale figure, a man with a kindly expression that seemed to be reaching out a crudely drawn but benevolent hand to place on her shoulder. A widow and her dead husband, obviously. The figure looked a little like Abraham Lincoln, but it was difficult to tell.

I touched the corner of *E* and felt nothing.

Then I stepped back to regard *C* and *D*.

I wished the windows had not been covered, because I would have liked to have consulted Horrible Hank. But there were no reflective surfaces in the room anywhere, no framed pictures under glass, and the globes of the gaslight were too brilliantly lit to be of any use. There wasn't even a pitcher of water, which would have been considerate as well as helpful.

"Hank," I called softly. "Are you anywhere nearby?"

No answer.

"Never around when I need you," I said.

So it was down to the war bride or the good-looking young man and the sorrowful ghost.

I reached out for the corner of *C*, feeling nothing.

"So much for proof of life after war," I said.

Then I touched *D*.

As soon as the pad of my forefinger met the paper, it was as if a bolt of lightning struck. The room exploded in a brilliant blue light, but there was no sound of thunder, only a vast silence that sucked me into it. My knees buckled and I could feel the floor rushing up to meet me, but I could do nothing to stop it. I felt myself hit with a thud and then everything went dark.

I don't know how long I was out. But when I came around, I had a name for the sorrowful ghost.

Angus Wright.

I went to the door and knocked three times.

19

After reminding me that I was still under oath, the judge asked if I had come to any conclusions.

"Yes," I said.

"Are any of the photographs you examined fakes?"

"Four of them," I said.

Decker, the prosecutor, exchanged an uneasy glance with Professor Bogardus, who was sitting in the crowd behind. The pack of reporters leaned forward, their pencils poised. Only Eureka Smith appeared not to be anxious to hear the outcome of my investigation; instead, he seemed a bit distracted, as if somebody were telling him a joke he'd already heard.

"That would leave one that is, in your estimation, an authentic spirit photograph," the judge said. "Please tell us which exhibit has passed your scrutiny?"

"Photograph *D*," I said.

The judge tapped a sheet of paper before him.

"According to the list I have here," he said, "that is a photograph of Andrew Jackson Miles taken by Eureka Smith. It is, in fact, the only Smith example in the lot. Exhibit *A* was made by Professor Bogardus, and the others were made by Mumler or his associates."

Decker was shuffling papers.

The reporters were scribbling furiously.

"Does that tally with your list, Mister Decker?" the judge asked.

"Yes, your honor," the prosecutor said meekly. "I should point out, however, that Miss Wylde had a twenty percent chance of choosing the Smith photo just by sheer chance. I would suggest that another test be arranged—"

"I think not," said the judge. "These were the conditions you agreed to beforehand, and I'm going to make you live with them, as hard as they might be to swallow now."

"Yes, your honor. May I question the witness?"

"Let's allow Mister Smith his turn, shall we?"

Eureka Smith nodded and stood up, smoothing his clothes. He thought for a full minute or more. He seemed about to ask a question, then thought better of it.

"I have nothing to ask, your honor."

"Very well. Proceed, Mister Decker."

Decker shot up out of his chair and approached the witness box.

"Please tell us exactly how you determined which photograph was Mister Smith's."

"That's not what I was asked to do," I said.

"Instead, I was asked to identify, if I could, any legitimate spirit photographs."

"Of course," he said. "But the question remains: How did you do it?"

"I don't know."

"You don't know?"

"Well, I don't know how to describe it," I said. "I wasn't sure if I could do it in the first place, having never been asked to do anything like it before."

I explained how I started just by looking at them, and then touching them, and about how I fainted and heard voices.

"You heard voices," he said, dismissively.

"Yes, sir."

"Do you hear voices often?"

"Yes, I hear yours now."

"You know what I meant, Miss Wylde."

"Sometimes."

"We have places for people who hear voices," he said.

"Churches?" I asked.

"Madhouses," he said.

The judge rapped his gavel.

"Enough of that, Mister Decker," he said. "You are to ask questions, not to debate or belittle the witness."

"Tell us about the voices you heard in the jury room."

"It's a little hard to describe," I said. "It's like being asleep, but not asleep. I first heard them back in Dodge City last year, when some cowboys who were angry with me tried to bury me alive in Boot Hill. I discovered I could talk to the dead, or at least hear them. It was the same there."

"You were buried alive?"

"My partner dug me out. Saved my life."

"Is this your usual form of detection?" Decker asked. "To lose consciousness and confer with the voices?"

"No, sir, it's not. Frankly, it's unusual. But I haven't fainted before on a case. You see, I haven't slept or eaten since leaving Dodge early Wednesday morning. I think that had something do with it."

Decker shook his head.

"This is all a bit much for us to believe," Decker said, playing to the jury. "The odds are not inconsiderable that you would have chosen the photograph by mere chance alone. For us to believe this display would require something more than chance—some concrete fact, something that would conclusively prove that the photograph in question was made by means unknown to man."

"There is," I said.

"I beg your pardon?"

"There is," I said. "I got something from the voices—"

"Stop right there," Decker said.

"—I heard the voices say—"

"A question has not been asked," Decker insisted.

"—a name."

The gavel came down again.

A murmur went through the crowd. The reporters were in paroxysms of note-taking. Decker looked as if somebody had thrown cold water on him.

"Just pause there if you would, Miss Wylde," the judge said. "Counsel, approach the bench. That means you, too, Mister Smith."

Decker ran to the bench. Smith shambled over.

There was much whispering between the judge and Decker, while Smith looked on, bemused. After several long minutes, the judge nodded.

Decker and Smith took their seats.

"The prosecution has asked for a recess of one week, which the court is disposed to grant," the judge said. "But looking at my calendar, I see that a week from today is the Fourth of July, and it is not only impractical to have court on that day, it would be disrespectful. In view of the national holiday, the court will recess for two weeks. This matter will resume at eight o'clock in the morning on Thursday, July 14. Miss Wylde, thank you for your service. You may step down and your services are no longer required. Court is adjourned."

20

Eureka Smith and I pushed our way through the phalanx of reporters and the crowd behind, all shouting questions. We raced out of the courtroom, down the hall, and took the flight of stone steps two at a time that led to the street.

"Really, I must have a bite to eat," I said.

Smith led me to Larimer Street, across the Cherry Creek Bridge, and into a neighborhood that seemed to be teeming with restaurants and hotels. He pulled me into a restaurant that advertised "ROCKY MOUNTAIN OYSTERS AND OTHER REFRESHMENTS." After we were seated, I told him that I hoped he didn't expect me to eat the oysters.

"You don't like seafood?" he asked.

"We call them calf fries in Dodge City," I said. "I assure you they've never seen the ocean. I don't eat them there, and I won't eat them here."

"Steak?"

"In Kansas they serve steak at breakfast, noon, and dinner."

"Ah," he said. "Then you are free to order what you like."

"What are you having?"

"I only eat fowl, of course."

Smith was a strange and awkward man.

"Of course," I said, not really wanting to know why.

The waiter came and took our order. Smith ordered a squab pie and a whiskey sour, and I had the pork roast and potatoes with a cup of tea.

"Thank you," Smith said. "I am in your debt."

"You are, at least for my expenses," I said. "Including this meal."

He nodded.

"Where did you get your unusual name?"

"Smith?" he asked.

"The other one."

"Like everyone else in Colorado at one time or another, I did some prospecting. Gold panning, mostly, shoveling bucket after bucket of dirt from the banks of the river near Fairplay. Panning it all out in a big metal pan and looking for color in the black sand that was left. After countless disappointing days of finding nothing, I discovered a shining golden object in one of the buckets and, holding the precious thing aloft, cried, 'Eureka!'"

He paused.

"Iron pyrite."

"Fool's gold."

"Yes," he said. "I should have known better. It was an octahedral pyrite cluster, the color of polished copper. My companions did not allow me to live it down. From that moment on, I have been Eureka Smith. But I have grown into the name, it seems."

"When did you take up the camera?"

"Shortly after the mining debacle," he said. "I proved somewhat more adept at turning a profit in silver than I ever had at gold."

"I don't understand."

"Photography is based on the light-sensitive properties of silver," he said. "All modern processes use some silver, typically in the form of silver nitrate or silver halide, to create the image."

"It must be difficult to learn."

"One can acquire the rudiments in a fortnight," he said. "To master it requires a lifetime."

"Have you?"

"I am still serving my apprenticeship," he said. Silence welled between us.

"What does the name Angus Wright mean to you?" I asked.

"Nothing," he said. "But the threat of revealing the name seemed to have a surprising effect on the prosecution. District Attorney Decker is a friend of Andrew Jackson Miles, so my guess is that the name has some connection to Miles."

"Why would it?"

Smith smiled.

"It is Councilman Miles, the mining baron and gubernatorial candidate, who is sitting in the photo you identified as genuine," Smith said.

"But what's the story?" I asked.

Smith shrugged.

"Miles commissioned a likeness so an engraving could be made for the newspapers," he said. "I have—or at least I had—some reputation here as a portrait artist of the first class. Privately, for a few friends and select clients, I had been experimenting with spirit photography, with unsatisfying results. This Miles portrait was not intended as an exercise in that pursuit, but merely as a tool for his campaign. When the results were not as he intended, he demanded the negative, and I refused, and told him I intended to display the image as a successful spirit photograph. He cried fraud and persuaded his friend, W. S. Decker, to file charges against me."

"There was no extortion involved?"

"He offered me a thousand dollars for the negative, but I was disinterested in selling. I offered him as many prints as he would like, at my usual fee, but he wanted the original destroyed."

"It is difficult to see how that resulted in a fraud case."

"Once he knew I was intent on exhibiting the photograph, his aim was to discredit me."

"And why did you represent yourself instead of hiring a lawyer?" I asked.

"It wasn't a matter of money, if that's what you're thinking."

"Then, what?"

"The legal community here knew Jackson Miles was connected to the case," he said. "Because he is likely to be the next governor of the state of Colorado, nobody was available for hire."

"The judge must not have been for hire."

"Judge Stone?" Smith asked. "Why no, he's a political agnostic."

"You must have believed rather fervently in your work, to go to all this trouble on principle."

"I take it earnestly," he said.

"You said your other attempts at spirit photography were unsuccessful," I said. "Did you do anything differently in producing this portrait?"

"Well, it was my first time photographing Jackson Miles," he said. "But I was experimenting with a mixture of gun cotton and magnesium powder, which produces a brilliant bluish white flash."

"Sounds dangerous."

"Not when handled correctly," he said. "But Miles acted as if the flash had somehow stung him. There was no evidence, however, that he was touched by a stray spark."

Our food came and I ate like a farmhand. Smith went about his squab pie methodically, as if he were calculating the volume of each bite. I drank my tea while I considered whether I could trust finding safe lodging in Denver. Then I remembered the book in my valise.

I took *Syrinx of the Seven Worlds* from its flour sack and asked Smith if he was familiar with it. He shook his head.

"It came from a library here in Denver," I said, opening the cover so he could see the stamp of *The Denver City and Auraria Reading Room and Library Association.* "It is some years overdue, and it's important that I return it—for a case I'm working on."

"I've never heard of it," he said. "But there is a library association and reading room near here, at about Fourth and Larimer streets. Perhaps they could direct you."

When Smith was finished, he settled the bill from a thick roll of greenbacks he carried in his pocket. Then he asked me what my expenses were.

"I'm not sure yet," I said. "It was nine dollars and four bits for a one-way ticket to Denver. There will be lodging, and meals, and, of course, the return trip."

Smith counted off three twenty-dollar notes.

"For expenses."

I heard Jack Calder's voice in my head.

"And then there's the matter of my fee," I said. "Twenty dollars."

"A day?"

"Per week," I said. "By the time I get back to Dodge, I will have lost the better part of a week."

Smith peeled off another note.

"You said on the stand that you have trouble charging people."

"You might have gotten off easy," I said, "if I had been asked first and not subpoenaed."

21

I took a room at the Centennial Hotel on the corner of Eighteenth and Black, just a couple of blocks from where we had dined on Larimer Street. It wasn't the fanciest hotel in Denver—that would be the Grand Central, I was told—but it was suitable for my need because it seemed safe and featured a bed.

I threw myself on the mattress and closed my eyes.

At least it was cooler in Denver, or at least it felt that way.

Denver was at the base of the Rocky Mountains and about 3,000 feet higher in elevation than Dodge City, making it a full mile above sea level. Not only was the temperature fifteen or twenty degrees cooler than Dodge, but the air was drier.

The sounds of the city came to me from the street below: the *clip-clop* of horses drawing wagons of beer and produce, the chatter of people on the sidewalk, the hum of the street trams, and the chug of locomotives and the booming of coupling cars from the half-dozen railway depots scattered about downtown.

I had forgotten how comforting those metropolitan sounds could be. With the city lullaby in my ears, soon I was fast asleep.

I am wandering from car to car, having succumbed to a kind of mindless boredom after exhausting all the possibilities for looking for the lost ticket. I find myself in the coffin car, and the widdershins are hauling a new box down the aisle.

They clumsily let it fall to the floor.

It hits with a crash and the wooden lid pops off. Out clatters dozens of Martini and Henry rifles. What are the rifles doing here, I ask? The widdershins giggle and taunt me with demonic grins, then begin packing the rifles back in the box. There's something about the Martini and Henry rifles that tugs at my memory, something I should know. Water witching. Yes, dowsing. I could dowse for the lost ticket. But where do I find a willow branch here?

"Best move along, miss," the white-gloved conductor says.

"Where?" I ask.

"Somewhere else," he says. "You can't stay here. You're distracting the widdershins."

"Why are they hauling rifles into the car?"

"Transfer of grave goods," he says. "They'll be unloaded at the next stop, or the one after." He glances at

his watch. "So many wars coming, it's hard to keep up with the demand."

I shiver.

"Do you know where I might find a willow branch?"

The conductor shakes his head.

"This ain't the botanical gardens. Watch your shins."

Another crate of rifles comes down the aisle, then careens toward me, and I step back to avoid being mangled. The widdershins laugh.

"They're beastly," I say.

"They do enjoy their work. Now, move along."

I step from the coffin car into one of the coaches. Except for a seat next to an old man, the car is full. I'm exhausted, so I sit. The old man stirs, obviously annoyed at having a seatmate.

"What year is it?" he asks.

"Pardon?"

"The year," he snaps. "Do you know the year?"

"Of course. It's 1878."

He shakes his head.

"Can't be," he says. "Impossible."

I cover my mouth as I yawn.

"I'm sorry, I'm just so tired."

"Tired?" he asks. "What do you know about tired?"

"A little."

"Very little. Just wait until you're my age."

"And what age is that?"

"Old."

"How old is old?"

"Forty years from now, that's old."

I lean forward and rest my head on my folded arms and drift off to wake wondering if I would feel old *when I was seventy—or if I would live long enough to find out.*

The sun was well up by the time I shook off my crazy dreams and crawled out of bed at the Centennial Hotel. I dressed and packed my things, not wanting to have the expense of another night in a hotel in a strange city.

On the street, the air was cool and crisp, and looming in the west I could see the snow-capped Rockies. I had never been in the mountains, anywhere, and these seemed strange and forbidding, a wall of rock whose scale I could not imagine.

I made my way the few blocks to the corner of Fourth and Larimer, looking for a sign that would indicate a library association nearby. Finding nothing, I crossed to the other corner, and scanned again. The result was the same—the buildings remained mute.

Finding myself standing in front of a tobacconist, I went inside and addressed the girl behind the counter. She was perhaps seventeen, with torrents of black hair and luminous brown eyes. Of course, nearly all of her customers were male.

"Sorry to trouble you," I said, "but do you know of a library located nearby?"

"Wouldn't you like a cigar?" she asked, leaning on the counter and smiling.

"No, thank you, I don't smoke. I understand there is a library association located in one of the buildings near this corner."

"This"—she said, picking up a fat cigar from a paste-paper box—"is a Brothers Upmann, rolled on the thighs of a beautiful *torcedora* in Havana." She placed the cigar beneath her nose and inhaled. "Umm," she said. "Delightful. Only twenty-five cents."

"Again, I don't smoke."

"Certainly there is a gentleman in your life who would enjoy this fine product," she said, holding it to the corner of her mouth as if she were puffing on it. "I've been here on this corner for two years, and I have become the confidant of many regular customers, some of whom actually read books instead of using them for doorstops. You could be among my circle of friends."

"Very well," I said. "You're extorting from me five times the price of a normal cigar, but I'll take it."

"Your gentleman will be grateful for your generosity," she said.

"I have no gentleman," I said.

"Pity," the girl said. "Soon, machines will take over the manufacture of smoking products and the magic will be gone—as well as the lovely cigar girls."

She rolled the cigar in a strip of wax paper, making a little tube. Then she twisted the ends and deftly tied them off with red ribbons.

"There," she said. "You will just have to make it a present to yourself."

I put my two bits on the counter.

"Thank you," she said, giving me her best smile.

"Is this the best cigar store in Denver?"

"It has the best clientele, if that's what you mean."

"Exactly. Are you familiar with a politician by the name of Jackson Miles?"

"Jacks," she said, and gave a wistful smile. "Very familiar."

"Jacks?"

"That's what his friends call him," she said. "His name on the ballot is always Andrew Jackson Miles—he added the Andrew because it draws more votes. He was born Jackson Miles, and his nickname forever is Jacks."

"And what do you think of this Jacks?"

"He's a city councilman," she said. "A powerful man, and certain to be our next governor. Quite fond of his cigars—and his cigar girls as well."

"I've seen a photo of him with one in hand."

"A girl?"

"A cigar," I said. "What can you tell me about his background and reputation?"

"You can find all of what you want in the columns of any of the leading city newspapers."

"I'm looking for information of a different sort," I said. "The kind that doesn't make it into the news columns of the leading papers."

She nodded and furrowed her brow in concentration.

"Now, here is what the baron prefers," she said, bringing out a fat cigar with a gold band from a cedar box behind the counter. "This is truly a cigar for a leader, made of only the best tobacco, and fermented as one would ferment the best wine. And it is a bargain, for only a dollar."

"A dollar? That would feed a family for a week."

"Not in Denver," the girl said.

"All right," I said, fishing a dollar note out of my pocket. "Here's a dollar. Keep the mile-high stogie. What do you know?"

"He's married, of course—"

"—of course—"

"—with three children, but he sometimes prefers the company of a certain dark-haired cigar girl. He talks often about his youthful adventures here in Denver, when he was a regular at the Elephant Corral, and later when he crossed the Mosquito Range to mine gold at California Gulch."

"In California?"

"No, it was the original mining camp near Leadville, a hundred miles over the mountains from here. They struck gold in Leadville in the sixties but really hit it big with silver a year ago. Baron Miles did plenty good for himself in gold, that's for sure. The silver boom has just made him richer."

"Has he made any opponents?"

"You mean like Fred Pitkin? They're both fighting for the Republican nomination, so naturally they're opponents. Whoever gets the nomination will be governor, because Colorado will elect a Republican. But Miles is so much more popular, Pitkin doesn't stand a chance."

"You seem to know a lot about politics."

"I only have to *act* dumb," she said.

"Does Miles have enemies that would do him bodily harm?"

"All rich and ambitious men have enemies."

"From his early days," I said.

"He had a partner at California Gulch," she said.

"What happened to him?"

"Miles said there was some kind of disagreement, and then the partner disappeared, so he guessed he just walked out. Found things too tough. It was pretty wooly in the early days, and still is, I guess."

"Do you remember this partner's name?"

"No," she said. "Something common, I think."

"I'm not buying another cigar."

"You don't need to because I really don't remember."

"Earlier you mentioned something about an elephant pen?"

"The Elephant Corral," she said. "It was famous during the gold boom. It stretched from Blake to Wazee streets, near the Cherry Creek Bridge, and it was a huge canvas-roofed hotel with a dirt floor. Sheets separated the rooms. It was a notorious spot for gamblers and thieves, and Miles has said it was the most exciting place he could imagine. He was twenty-one and had come from a small town in Ohio and fell in with a bad lot, and was forced to hurt a lot of people but never killed anyone. From there, he set out to make his fortune at California Gulch."

"A real Ragged Dick," I said.

"Pardon?

"Horatio Alger," I said. "Ragged Dick is one of the characters in his novels. You know, hard work pays off? I was making a joke."

"Oh," the cigar girl said. "I just read the newspapers."

"Anybody around the Elephant Corral now that might remember Miles?"

"It burned down in 1863," she said. "And most people were just passing through, anyway, on their way to the gold fields."

"That's unfortunate," I said. "Did he say anything to you about the spirit photograph case?"

She shook her head.

"I read about it, but he didn't discuss it with me."

"Thanks for your time," I said.

I picked up the Brothers Upmann cigar and stuck it in my breast pocket.

"Don't you want to know about the library?"

I had completely forgotten why I had stopped in the first place.

"Yes, of course."

"Over on the opposite corner, 405 Larimer. Second floor, above the hardware store."

"I don't know how I missed it."

"They took down the sign," she said, "because they are closing down."

"What on earth for?"

"Guess cigars are more popular in Denver than books."

22

There was a narrow flight of stairs beside the hardware store. At the top, the stairs opened onto a spacious landing with several offices with frosted glass doors. There was an assayer and an attorney, a dentist and an engineer, and at the end of the hall, in ghost letters where the name had been removed from the window with turpentine, the Denver Library Association.

I knocked, and the unlatched door swung open a crack.

"Hello?" I called.

"The reading room is closed," a man called. "For good."

"Then I've arrived none too soon," I said, opening the door a bit more.

A man came marching toward the door, looking as if he intended on slamming it shut. He was in his shirtsleeves, with his suspenders hanging from his waist, and with a blue marking crayon over his right ear.

"Could I have a moment of your time?"

"I told you, we're closing down," he said. "I'm crating up all of these books and trying to mark what's in each of them so the crates don't get mixed up. They're all going to the Board of Education, for the benefit of the students. There are six hundred volumes here, and I'd like to get this done by the end of the day."

"That's an ambitious plan," I said. "Why did this task fall upon you?"

"Because I'm the treasurer, or was the treasurer, of this failed civic experiment," he said. I raised my eyebrows, waiting for him to introduce himself. "I'm sorry, my name is Charles B. Patterson. I'm an agent for a bank down the street, but today I'm just a combination stock and delivery boy."

"Miss Ophelia Wylde," I said. "Here on business, I'm afraid."

"Charmed, Miss Wylde."

He opened the door and I stepped into what was once a very comfortable reading room. He indicated a pair of leather chairs, and I took the one closest to the window. It has become my habit not to sit facing the light because it makes it difficult to read expressions.

"What kind of business?" he asked.

"Detective business," I said. "My agency is in Dodge City, and I'm working on a case that involves what appears to be a suicide but may prove to be murder instead."

"That sounds quite serious. What led you here?"

"This book," I said, removing *Syrinx of the Seven*

Worlds from my bag. "It seemed quite important to the owner, the victim in the case, and there is a stamp on the title page indicating that it was the property of the library association of Denver City and Auraria. It is quite overdue, by some eighteen years."

He took the book, looked at the stamp, and smiled.

"This is not our association," he said.

I cursed in French—to myself.

"But we did inherit the records of that association."

I had sworn too soon.

"Would it be possible for me to take a look?"

"Of course," he said. "If only I can find the right box. I've tried to label everything properly, but there is the press of time, and the enormity of the task."

He walked to the back of the room and began moving crates of books around, searching.

"Did you know any of the principals of this earlier library association?"

"No," he said. "It was all before my time, back in the days when Denver City was untamed. The association didn't last long, as I recall. Only a year or so, and there wasn't another library until ours was formed in 1873."

"Well, you lasted five years. That's something."

"Here it is," he said, bringing out a ledger. He blew the dust from the cover and opened it to the first page. "Your association seems to have been formed in the winter of 1859 and 1860, to create a circulating library for subscribers. The first recorded meeting is of February 10, 1860, and it lists the mission of the association."

He handed me the ledger.

Whereas, the want of a place of resort where citizens of our towns can meet during their leisure hours for the purpose of gaining information, improving their minds and engaging in social conversation and enjoyment, has long been and still is felt in our midst; and, Whereas, experience has proven by the establishment of reading rooms in other cities, that they tend to both mental and moral cultivation—Therefore, we the undersigned, resolve to form ourselves into an Association, and swear a prime understanding of the penalty for infidelity.

On the following pages were the names of the subscribers, who paid dues of fifty cents per month to belong. There were ninety-nine names in the ledger, numbered according to a system that I guessed corresponded to their date of joining.

I ran my finger down the list of names and found:

13. Angus Wright.

"How strange," I said.
A little farther down, there was:

23. Jackson Miles.

"Is it proving a help or a hindrance?"

"Two mysteries become one," I said. "And more complex."

And on the next page, this:

29. John Shear. Lynched and hung for horse stealing.

"Why would the library association note the lynching of one of its members?" I asked.

"Oh, the Shear entry," he said. "It was quite a scandal. Even I've heard about that. After a secret tribunal condemning a horse-stealing ring, Shear was hauled from his bed in Auraria City by vigilantes, taken to the bank of the Platte River below the Larimer Street crossing, and hanged from a cottonwood tree. A note was found pinned to his chest that read, *'This man was hung. It was proved he was a horse thief.'*"

This was similar to the note that Molly Howart said was pinned to the ghost hanging in her front room.

"Who were members of this grim tribunal?"

"Nobody knows," he said. "Or at least, nobody's talking."

"I still find it remarkable that it was necessary to note his end in the association's ledger."

I ran down the remaining pages of names, but none of them looked familiar. Also, there was something peculiar about the list of names. Although there were only ninety-nine names listed, the number entries went to 125; there were seventeen blank spaces, including, for example, the numbers 43 and 59. Why, if the names were written in the order members had joined, were numbers skipped?

I asked Patterson and he said he didn't know.

"Does the name Angus Wright mean anything to you?"

"No, sorry," he said. "The only names on the list I'm familiar with are Shear, because of the hanging story, and Jackson Miles, obviously."

"Obviously. What about this language in the preamble, about the 'prime penalty for infidelity.' That seems a bit out of place in this kind of document, don't you think?"

He shrugged.

"Books were even more valuable in camp than they are now."

Even though two, or perhaps three, of the names on the list were immediately significant, I knew there might be more. It would be necessary to have the list.

"May I borrow the ledger?"

Patterson scratched the back of his neck.

"It is a historic document going back to the founding of the city," he said. "I'm not sure I should let it go back to—where did you say you were from?—Kansas."

"Perhaps I could make a copy, under your supervision."

"Yes, I suppose that would be all right," he said. "But I think you should return that book you have."

"The Gresham book?"

"It technically belongs to the school district now, just as our association inherited all of the assets of the former library," Patterson said. "It appears to have been quite an expensive book, and the Board of Education no doubt could use it."

Men. Why did they turn everything into a horse trade?

I considered for a moment. Although *Syrinx of the Seven Worlds* appeared to be connected to the ledger entry of the hanged man—and the ghost no doubt was the unlucky John Shear—I desperately needed the full list of names. In addition, the book was written by a lunatic, the content did not seem key to the case, and the volume was exceedingly haunted. If one could help a restless ghost cross over by taking care of unfinished business, couldn't you bring peace to an overdue and very haunted library book by returning it, as closely as possible, to its source?

"All right," I said, handing over the book. "You have a deal."

"Done," Patterson said. He took the book and threw it into a crate near the back of the room, then marked the crate with the blue crayon. I hoped no poor student of the Denver Board of Education perusing the school library one night would be confronted with the hanged ghost of John Shear.

Still, I was curiously sad to part with the strange book.

Patterson continued to work, stacking crates on top of the one that contained *Syrinx*.

Because of the matter of cost, I still had not assembled a detective kit with the necessary aids, so I could not yet begin my copying.

"May I borrow a sheet of paper and a pencil?"

I sat in the leather chair with the good light behind me and as quickly and accurately as I could made my copy of the preamble and the list of names, including the unfilled numbered lines. While I worked, Patterson continued to crate books, and I suppose a good hour had passed when the shadow of a man darkened the frosted glass of the reading room door.

23

The door swung open without the customary knock, revealing a man whose likeness I had only seen before in the spirit photo at the courthouse—Andrew Jackson Miles.

Miles was standing with his feet planted, but his head down and his hat in one hand. The other held a cigar, and its smoke uncoiled from his fist like a snake. He was perhaps forty years old, and his most remarkable feature was his thick black hair, as straight and as coarse as the mane of a thoroughbred.

He gave a sly smile.

"Miss Wylde," he said.

"Councilman Miles," I said. "Or should I call you 'Jacks'?"

The ledger hid my right hand as I stuffed my copied list of names into my bag.

"Only my friends call me that."

"I've heard as much, from the cigar girl on the street corner," I replied. "She must have alerted you, because nobody else knew of my presence here in this about-to-be-shuttered reading room. Sad, isn't it?"

"What is sad?" he asked.

"The closing of a library for the public," I said. "What else?"

"Councilman Miles," Patterson said, rushing forward with his hand outstretched. "It's an honor to meet you, sir."

Instead of shaking Patterson's hand, Miles placed his hat in his hand.

"Find a place for that, will you? And this."

He handed over a cane, a wicked black thing topped by a bright silver knob with his initials, *AJM*. He must have been holding the cane in the same hand as his hat, because I didn't notice it until he handed it to Patterson.

The cane went into a basket near the door, and the hat atop the cane.

"I'm sorry," Patterson said. "We're short on creature comforts, considering."

"What's your name?" Miles asked.

Patterson told him.

"I never forget a name," Miles said. "And you will never remember I was here. Now, go."

"Sir? I have work to do."

"It's time for you to take a break from whatever you were doing," Miles said. "A long break. Don't come back until tomorrow."

"But—" Patterson stammered a bit. "But I don't think I should leave the room unattended, or to leave you—I beg your pardon, sir—or to leave you alone with Miss Wylde, considering your odd demeanor."

Miles turned slowly to look at Patterson.

"We will attend to the room. And Miss Wylde will be quite safe."

The way he said *safe* made my breath catch in my chest.

"Yes," I forced myself to say. "Don't worry, Mister Patterson. Everything will be well looked after. And I thank you for your help."

Patterson hesitated.

"Go on," I said. "Truly, I'm fine."

He nodded, then stepped toward the door.

"Close it," Miles said.

Patterson did, and the closing of the reading room door seemed terribly ominous, even more threatening than when the jury room was locked from the outside. Miles stood looking at me for many seconds while dust motes drifted between us in the shaft of sunlight that poured over my right shoulder.

"Why is your intention to ruin me?" he asked.

"It is my experience," I said, "that people are quite capable of ruining themselves with no help from me."

"Clever," he said.

He walked over, dragged the other leather chair away from the shaft of sunlight, and placed it nearly arm to arm with mine, in a manner so we faced one another.

"You are something more than I expected," he said.

"What did you expect?"

"Not you," he said. "Some well-meaning but inconsequential woman who believes in humbug and speaks nonsense, most likely. Or a Spiritualist who babbles about the everlasting sunshine of Summerland and how happy are the dead there, but has nothing to say about the hard material things, the real things, before her. But certainly not you."

"I am pleased to disappoint."

"Decker is an idiot," he continued, then took a malodorous draw on the cigar. "He assured me that your coming to Denver could be turned to our advantage, that your expert testimony would be laughable and contribute to the impression that poor chicken-eating Eureka Smith was a fool or a charlatan or both. Even by chance, he said, there was only a one-in-five chance of you picking the Smith photograph. Those are good odds. I took them—why not? Those are house odds. But not only did you beat the house, you busted it."

"I do not play games of chance, Councilman."

"All the worse," he said. "You played with a marked deck, and the risk was mine."

"There was trickery. And any harm was incidental to my task before the court."

"I find it difficult to believe that this wasn't engineered by a third party," he said. "Fred Pitkin, no doubt. Damn that old Connecticut Yankee; he came to Colorado for his health and is ruining mine. Whatever he's paying, I can beat it."

"Nobody's paying me."

"You're working for someone."

"I work for my clients. At present, sir, I have only one—a widow in Dodge City to whom I must report shortly."

He stared at me, holding the cigar loosely in his right hand. The ash was growing long and I was afraid it would drop on the arm of the chair and burn the leather.

"You could be charged with perjury," he said.

He tapped the ash to the floor and brought the cigar to his lips.

"I don't see how," I said.

"A simple matter," he said. "A word to my friend, United States District Attorney Decker. If not perjury, then obstruction of justice. Or tampering with evidence. Any felony will do."

"How quickly you resort to threat."

"No threat," he said. "I'm protecting my reputation by urging you to do the honorable thing and reconsider the path you've taken. My goal is corrective in nature, a kindly uncle asking an errant niece to mend her ways."

I folded my arms over the records of the old library.

"May I?" he asked, indicating the ledger.

"Of course," I said.

"A relic of a halcyon era," he said, turning the pages. "Did you find anything of interest? My name is listed, of course."

"Along with about a hundred others," I said. "Mister Patterson pointed it out. As a whole, the ledger meant little to me."

"Then why were you asking my cigar girl about me?"

"I was on my way to the reading room here on another matter," I said. "I stopped to ask directions. Because you were identified as the man in the photograph, I was naturally curious. You might say it was just the kind of talk that women engage in to pass the time."

"And I suppose you simply have a taste for expensive cigars?"

"I suppose I do."

"It matches your outfit," he said. "This other matter . . ."

"A private matter, related to the client I mentioned in Dodge City."

He nodded.

"If you don't mind, I think I'll take this with me," he said, patting the ledger.

"It means nothing to me," I said.

And I doubted that Patterson would find the sand to object.

He stood and took a last puff of his cigar, which had grown very short.

"You haven't gotten what you really came here for, have you?"

"And what would that be?" he asked, smoke whistling through his teeth.

"The name I nearly spoke in court," I said. "The bluster and the bullying, that was just to see what I'm made of, to see if you could turn me or if I would be a problem. I turned into a problem, so you've decided not to ask about the name, for fear of tipping your hand in the direction of the secret you are desperately trying to keep."

"That's absurd," he said.

He gathered his hat and cane from the basket near the door.

"Who is Angus Wright?" I asked.

He dropped the butt of the cigar on the floor and ground it out with his heel, then glanced at me with eyes that were as hard as marbles.

"I don't know anyone by that name," he said.

If he was lying, he was very good at it. But then, he would be—he was a politician.

24

It's only a hundred miles from Denver to Lead-ville, but it seemed like a thousand. For seventeen dollars, I'd bought a ticket on the Spotswood & McClellan Stage Line (which had the government mail contract) and was assured a "smooth ride" because it was "the best time of year to travel."

Smooth and *best* proved relative.

For the next forty-eight hours, I was packed inside a Concord coach with eight other passengers, all men twice my size (there were another four or five clinging to the top of the coach, as well as a ziggurat of bags and trunks). I was jostled about as if I were the ball on a roulette wheel, landing first in one lap and then another. The driver pressed the six-horse team as if the devil himself were on our tail, and stopped every ten or fifteen miles to change horses at stage stops that were remarkable for their inhospitality.

We spent a few hours at a stage stop that featured

a meal that was unrecognizable by any civilized standard and offered a coffin-sized tract of puncheon for a nap. I refused the meal, save for coffee, and spent the time with my back against the wall, listening to the hellish symphony made by the snores of my fellow travellers. Come dawn, there was another meal in name only, and we were packed back into our cradle of misery, where my companions declared what an easy trip it had been and that the first of July was truly the best time to cross the mountains to Leadville.

No railroad had yet reached Leadville, but in the wake of the discovery of rich lodes of silver there the year before, both the Santa Fe and the Denver & Rio Grande were fighting to see who would be the first to lay track up the Arkansas River valley to the country's newest and richest boomtown. Another railway had begun to lay tracks west of Denver, but so far had made it less than twenty miles. Everybody wanted to get to Leadville, and fast, but for the present, my only route was by stagecoach.

The only thing that made the trip bearable was that I was ascending those mysterious and forbidding mountains I had seen from afar while on the streets of Denver. I grew up along the Mississippi, at just a hundred or so feet above sea level; Dodge City is only at about 1,200; and Denver was the highest I'd ever been. But at Weston Pass, I was higher still.

The driver said we were at an altitude of 12,000 feet. That beat the mile-high city of Denver

by more than a mile. We were up above the tree
line, on a barren saddle where swaths of snow still
hugged the shadows, and the air was cool enough
to make me glad I was inside the coach. There
was only one other pass across the Mosquito
Range, the line of saw-toothed peaks that was the
primary obstacle to travel between Leadville and
points east; the other was the impossibly high
Mosquito Pass, at more than 13,000 feet, which
was only passable—some of the time—on foot or
hooves.

We had followed a fork of the South Platte
up the side of the mountains and had been rewarded with views of crystal lakes and alpine
meadows. Now that we were at the pass, things
began to change; for one, there was a toll road at
the pass, with the gatekeeper charging one dollar
and fifty cents for each wheeled conveyance. The
road here was corduroyed with timbers, to allow
passage in bad weather and to keep the ruts from
growing so deep as to break a wheel, but it made
the ride teeth-rattling. There was so much traffic
over the pass—horses and wagons and even
people on foot packing bedrolls and shovels—
that a constant cloud of dust marked the pass. I
had never seen such a mass of mixed humanity
on the move, intent on a single destination and
carrying unbelievable loads, against such a vast
and difficult terrain, that it reminded me of an
army of ants.

In addition to affording views that would defy
description to my neighbors back in Dodge, the

two-day journey allowed me time to think. I had purchased the ticket on impulse, while I was still spoiling from the verbal fencing with Council-man Miles, thinking that his secret must lie in California Gulch. There had been no waiting, be-cause the stage line ran two coaches a day to Leadville, each way, and I promptly climbed aboard one that was ready to depart.

Upon reflection, it was a logical, if risky, move (I was insufficiently prepared for the cost of the journey—I'd already spent nearly a quarter of the money that Eureka Smith had given me). If anybody could tell me the story of Angus Wright and "Andrew" Jackson Miles, it would be some-body who had been in the Leadville district from its gold rush days.

The secret had to lie in the list of names and blank lines from the library association ledger, the hanged horse thief John Shear, and the al-leged self-hanging of poor Charlie Howart. It was all too coincidental to be the product of chance. But what was the connection? Why had Howart hidden the strange and haunted book, *Syrinx of the Seven Worlds*? And did he suspect that he was going to be murdered when he bought the insur-ance policy? Who had murdered Howart and tied the strange knot in the rope from which the body dangled?

The fact that Howart was murdered appeared more certain, considering *Syrinx* led me to the library ledger, and the ledger contained the odd entry about Shear.

It seemed reasonable to exclude any Dodge City natives from the list of suspects for the murder. He had only been in Dodge for a year, having come from Newton, where he and Molly had married some five years before. Nothing that had transpired in Kansas suggested a past that was worthy of either a haunting or a homicide.

Of the strangers in Dodge City around the time of Howart's murder, I personally knew of only three—and all three were candidates for suspicion. There was the Sky Pilot, the mudlark, and Clement Hill.

The Sky Pilot appeared mad, but might have a reason for giving such an impression. He certainly was strong, as I had discovered when he grasped the front of my shirt, and his age was sufficient that he might have shared a past with Charlie Howart. Also, he had taken flight from the China Doll not long after the body was found.

The mudlark—Bruce Chatwin by name, the man I met on the banks of the Arkansas River at Dodge—seemed unconnected, but he did say he was bound for Leadville. If he were on a murder mission, however, why would he announce a destination that would prove connected to a greater mystery? I'm sure Chatwin was telling the truth about growing up in England, because an accent like his would have been difficult to fake, and an unnecessary bit of theater to boot. He was too young to have been a participant in the events in Denver during 1860—he would have been little more than a child—but he might have been hired by someone who was involved. But he said he hadn't come to America until 1863, when he was hired as a draft replacement for a rich man's son in the Union Army.

Clement Hill, the salesman for the Western Mutual Life Assurance Company, was more than old enough to have been a contemporary. He appeared to value numbers above all else, which was in keeping with the style of the library ledger, and he dealt with death (albeit in an abstract way) on a daily basis. Was it possible he could have sold Charlie Howart a policy, killed him and dressed the scene, then denied the widow's claim by citing the suicide exemption? Perhaps, but remotely so. Also, he did not appear to be a large or fit enough man to haul Howart's body up. It was possible, I told myself, that I was including him on the list of suspects just because I didn't like him. But I wasn't ready to exclude him from the list, at least not yet.

As the stage bounced along, descending into the upper Arkansas River valley, we came to a place called Rocky Point, where the road became a narrow path that whipsawed between a rock face on one side and a sheer drop on the other. Our driver, still feeling the flames of hell upon his neck, dropped a rear wheel off the edge and, for a moment, the coach seemed about to plunge to oblivion, then jerked forward to find the road— and left my stomach floating somewhere behind. We hadn't gone more than thirty yards before meeting a coach going the other way, and I realized that only a matter of seconds separated a safe passage from a spectacular and undoubtedly fatal wreck that would have made news all the way back to Dodge City.

My first glimpse of Leadville was through a picket of pine trees. The city was strewn across the valley, a motley assortment of tents and cabins and raw-lumbered boxes, with a cluster of substantial-looking buildings going up in the center of town. Everything was new and arranged in some strange geometry, and all of it reflected the late-afternoon sun, especially the buildings of freshly sawn lumber, which shone like pale gold. The appearance reminded me of Eureka Smith's description of the octahedral crystal he had plucked from the bucket.

As the coach descended into the valley, the view got better, or at least clearer, because there were no trees left standing. All of it had gone into the building of Leadville, or down into the mines. The valley itself seemed featureless of any natural thing, having been scoured right down to dirt and rock; even the channel for the Arkansas River, which admittedly was only a stream this close to the headwaters, had been diverted in several places, to feed the mining or smelting operations. In the places where there wasn't a building or a mine operation, there were smoldering mounds of trash or rusting industrial debris.

The effect, once having seen the breathtaking views on the other side of Weston Pass, was disorienting, as if one were witnessing the desecration of a great cathedral.

Humanity surged through the mud streets of Leadville and over her trash-strewn slopes, a mob driven by greed and ambition, while the clang of steel on rock stung the crystal air. Crude timber tripods supported the tackle for buckets that went down open shafts on hemp ropes. The ropes were wound around a wooden drum, driven by horses walking in circles, which hoisted the ore up. There were several hundred of these wooden tripods—which I later learned were called *headframes*—across the valley.

Most headframes were rough affairs, like a tripod of telegraph poles, but here and there in the valley were stout blocky frames of considerable size, the marker of a well-financed corporate operation. There was all manner of complicated equipment beside these headframes, including boilers that looked like they belonged to steam locomotives, and pipes snaking everywhere. From the shafts came the constant rumble of the ore buckets and the shriek of some kind of mechanized demon. This was the Burleigh drill, I learned, a 250-pound jack-mounted monster driven by compressed air. It could drill a four-foot hole into the hardest rock in five minutes, twenty times faster than any human being could. Into the pattern of holes bored by the drill in a rock face at the end of a drift were inserted red sticks of dynamite, universally known as "giant" blasting powder, made from a volatile mixture of nitroglycerin and gun cotton. The blasts were set off at the end of the work day so the dust and fumes would have time to settle before the broken pieces of rock, called *muck*, were cleared out and the process could begin anew. Being late in the afternoon, a few muffled *thuds* reverberated across the valley.

I stepped off the coach in the middle of Leadville with my head spinning, both from the altitude and the cacophonous chaos around me. Behind me, my fellow passengers shouted and argued about the ownership of various articles being handed down from the top of the Concord. There were some sharp words and a pistol was drawn to settle the matter, but I did not hear it fired.

Clutching the valise to my stomach, I made my way to what seemed the most respectable establishment in the camp, a clapboard building with a sign proclaiming CITY HOTEL. It appeared to be general store, saloon, restaurant, and hotel. It was in a row of buildings that approached the urban in materials and workmanship, including a small building of brick that proclaimed itself to be a bank.

I climbed the wooden steps to the hotel, stepped over a miraculously sleeping dog in the doorway, and approached the desk.

"A private room, please."

"We have rooms for rent, but ain't none of them private," the man said. "We have six beds to a room, not counting sleeping space on the floor. I doubt you would be interested in sharing a room with nine or ten miners, miss."

"No, I've just had a similar experience on the coach from Denver."

"The miners wouldn't allow it, anyway."

"Ah, what do you mean?"

I felt insulted and deficient at once.

"They would insist on you having the room to yourself, even though they had paid," he said. "They are a rough lot, but most will treat every woman as good as a princess."

"That must be a waste in a city sorely lacking in royalty. Are there other hotels in town?"

"There are, but this is the top of the heap," the man said.

"I see. Say, were you around here in the old days?"

"You mean the silver strike last year?"

"No, I mean the gold rush."

"Nope," he said. "I've only been here since May."

"Can you think of anyone to ask about the California Gulch days?"

"What for?"

"I'm just looking for some history," I said.

"Well, you might try Horace Tabor. He's the mayor and postmaster of Leadville, but he started in the gulch. His store is three doors down.

There's a miner's meeting tonight, so you'd better catch him in the next hour or so."

I walked down to Tabor's Mercantile, a wood frame building that had actually been given a coat of white paint. Inside, the store was surprisingly well-appointed, with full shelves and glass display cases and barrels of apples, crackers, and pickles. Against one wall, however, there was an impressive selection of mining tools, including denim work clothes, candles, chisels, picks, and sledgehammers. In the far corner, near a stove, were a couple of men playing checkers while others watched. The store was dealing with a rush of business, as the miners stopped for groceries after work, and it took me a few minutes to work my way up to the counter.

"May I get you something?" the woman behind the counter asked.

There were two other clerks at work, both men, but this woman was in obvious charge. She was forty-five, or close to it, but her hair was still dark and in ringlets around her forehead. She wore glasses, behind which were bright inquisitive eyes, and her manner was confident.

"Yes," I said, suddenly overtaken by hunger. I asked for some bread and cheese, so that I could make sandwiches. While she went about slicing and wrapping my things, I walked with her down the counter, and asked if she knew if Mayor Tabor was in.

"I should hope so," she said. "He's my husband. He's in the back, tending to some postal business.

More and more mail arrives from Denver every day. Why do you ask?"

"I was hoping that he would be able to share with me the history of California Gulch," I said.

"He will bore you silly," she said. "He is one of those men who can't keep a narrative to save his life. Oh, he starts out strong, but things get tangled up along the way, and he arrives at someplace that nobody could see when the story started, including him. So, you have to ask the question all over again."

"I understand," I said.

"If you want to know about California Gulch, you should ask me," she said. "I was with him all the way from . . . well, all the way from Maine, actually. Then several brutal years in Kansas, where we tried to make a go of homesteading, and then to Denver, and finally to the gulch, in 1860."

"Yes, I would love to talk to you about it."

"Are you writing a history?"

"No," I said. "But history does figure into my theme."

I told her who I was, and about the agency in Dodge City, but was light on details of what led me to Denver and then Leadville. She said her name was Augusta Tabor. We exchanged "pleased-to-meet-you's," then she handed over the tightly wrapped bread and cheese.

"Let's see," she said, wiping her brow. "That will be one dollar and twenty-five cents."

"Oh, so much?"

"I wish it were less, for your sake," she said,

"but Leadville produces wealth, not food. Most of everything has to be hauled in, some of it a hundred miles up the mountains in freight wagons, and our cost isn't cheap. And, dear, this is a boomtown."

I smiled and paid her.

"I'd love to chat, but—" she said, indicating the line of men behind me.

"Of course," I said, gathering my purchases.

"Perhaps I could call on you later, and we can chat about local history. It's pleasant to have another woman in town who is interested in something other than relieving miners of their wages," she said. "Where are you staying?"

"I don't know," I said, moving toward the door. "It seems a challenge to find a private room."

"Stay here," she said. "Come back at eight."

I turned and gave her a smile.

On the street, I searched for a place to sit and eat my dinner, but there were even more men than before, and they were all in a hurry. It was difficult to navigate in such crowded conditions, so I stopped at the first place that afforded a bit of room, a flat-topped rock between two buildings. The rock was about the size of my desk back at the agency, and had apparently been used to try out some drilling equipment, because it was peppered with bore holes that ranged in depth from one inch to a foot. I climbed on the rock, sat cross-legged, and spread my meal before me. I tore a piece of bread from the loaf with my hands, but wished I had a knife for the cheese, which I was forced to mangle with my fingers. I added a pocket knife to the list of things for my detection bag. I would need the knife to sharpen pencils anyway.

I ate and immediately felt better, but soon wished I had something to drink. There were rain barrels at the corners of the businesses, many with cups or ladles attached by a piece of string, but I wasn't thirsty enough to use a public utensil. I packed up the rest of my food, stowed it in my valise, and started for a saloon across the street— The Parisian—when I heard a voice I knew.

"Friends! Thirst not for wickedness, but for every word that falls from the Savior's lips. Come away with me to the river, and we will bathe in the waters of righteousness."

The Sky Pilot was standing in front of The Parisian, arms outstretched, Bible in hand. The book seemed a few chapters lighter. His clothes and beard were filthy. He wasn't as painfully thin as he had been in Dodge, but his eyes were just as wild.

I stepped back, into some shadows cast by the corner of a building, but kept watching.

"Sir," he said, grasping the sleeve of a working-man who was about to enter The Parisian. "You will find no joy inside, only the heartbreak that is at the bottom of every bottle of hard drink."

"For the love of God," the man said, shaking himself loose. He continued inside, shaking his head.

"You, then," the Sky Pilot said, grasping an-other patron by the elbow. This man looked as if he were a driller or a driller's helper, and his biceps coiled beneath his greasy shirt. "Renounce drunken—"

The man drove his right fist into the side of the Sky Pilot's jaw. The sound was like that of a bat stroking a leather-covered baseball, and the preacher's head snapped around as if hit by a bat as well. The big man laughed as the Sky Pilot staggered for a few steps and then dropped to his knees.

Then, slowly, like a ship capsizing, he dropped and rolled over onto his back, the Bible clutched to his chest.

The crowd of men in the street pressed on, as if nothing unusual had happened. They didn't even break their stride. Nobody stopped to help the preacher, or to inquire about his health. Those bound for the saloon simply stepped—or jumped—over his body in their haste to get inside the door.

A trio of young boys had been watching from the side of the road, and now they ran out and leaned over the Sky Pilot. The oldest boy was ten or twelve, and he stared so intently at the preacher's face that I thought for a moment that he was going to help him. But then the boy drew his right foot back and kicked the preacher in the ribs, laughing like a little jackal. The other boys soon imitated their leader, little brogans being driven repeatedly into the side of the poor man.

"Stop that!" I shouted, making my way across the road. "Boys, stop!"

The kicking ceased, but they stood their ground and stared at me defiantly.

"Where are your mothers?" I asked.

This was not the right question to ask.

"Forget you," the oldest boy said, although the word he used was not *forget*. "My mother's a whore."

"Yeah," another of the boys said.

"You're hurting him."

"I'll stop if you give me a dime," the older boy said.

"And give you an incentive to hurt him, so next time you can ask for a quarter to stop kicking him?"

"What's it to you?"

"How would you like being kicked by some-body bigger than you?"

"I'm smaller than him," the boy said, confused.

"Yes, but I'm bigger than you," I said. "And if I catch you abusing somebody like this again, I'm going to kick the living snot out of all of you until somebody pays me fifty cents to stop. Now, scram."

The boys took off.

I grabbed the Sky Pilot by the back of the collar and dragged him over to the side of The Parisian's porch, enough out of the way so he wouldn't get stepped on. I knelt and made sure he was breathing. His eyes fluttered as I put the book beneath his hands.

"Suffer the little children," he said.

"Suffer, indeed."

"Don't I know you, sister?"

He reached out and grasped the lapel of my jacket.

Alarmed, I knocked his hand away.

"Don't do that," I said. "I'm not helping you again."

I opened the valise, took out the loaf of bread, and tore off a hunk.

"You eat this," I said. "Not pages from the book. This."

I placed the bread in his right hand.

"I'm not helping you again," I said. "You're on your own."

No response.

"Do you understand me, Martin?"

He blinked.

"Is that my name?"

"I have it on good authority," I said.

I gathered my things in the valise and was about to stand, then hesitated.

"You're not a killer, are you?"

"We're all sinners," he said.

"No, I mean literally. Did you kill Charlie Howart?"

"Who?"

"Howart," I said. "Charles Howart."

He shook his head.

"You're not just pretending to be crazy, are you?"

"No," he said slowly. "There are still moments when, as if the scales have fallen from my eyes, I know I am quite mad. But those moments are forgotten in the rush and everlasting glory of God's word. I am a voice crying in the wilderness."

I stood.

"When those moments come," I said, "try hard to remember where home is. Return to your family. No more preaching until then, please. Go home, or you're going to die in the wilderness."

25

The mercantile was closed, but through the window I could see the glow of a lamp at the back of the store. Augusta Tabor was sitting beside the lamp, concentrating on some material before her, a pencil in her hand.

I rapped gently.

She came forward and unbarred the door.

"I'm glad you came," she said.

"I'd be sleeping on the street if I didn't," I said.

"You'd freeze in those clothes," she said. "It can get a little chilly here at night, even in the middle of summer."

"It will be a nice change from Kansas," I said. "I can hardly sleep, it's so hot at night."

She replaced the bar after I'd entered and then led me toward the back.

"I was just going over some accounts," she said. "It never ceases to amaze me how much work is involved in running a store, and this is our third—we have one in Oro City and another at

Buckskin Joe, another mining camp. Horace has a talent for making deals, but when it comes to the books, I prefer to do it myself. My head is better for numbers than his."

She leaned over and blew out the lamp.

"Sleeping quarters are above," she said, leading me up a flight of stairs that already had a light at the top. The stairs opened on a sitting area that was tastefully arranged, with a little table and padded chairs and the other things one would expect in a comfortable home.

"We have a home nearby," she said, "but business has been so brisk that I seldom get to it, so I make do here. There's a sleeping room just on the other side there, nothing fancy, just a bed and a nightstand. Horace is quite the politician and is always putting up some visiting official or another, and bragging to them about how he wants to build an opera house in town. An opera house, can you imagine? So, it's my turn to show a little kindness to a new friend."

"Thank you again," I said.

"Horace is still at the miner's meeting—there is at least a crisis a day in a boomtown—so it will be just us. Would you care for a cup of tea?"

We sat in the padded chairs and drank tea, and she told me about life in California Gulch in 1860.

At the time, she said, the area was still Kansas Territory. It is strange now to think of a Kansas gold rush, but that's what it was. A series of strikes, beginning in 1858 with the Pikes Peak rush, brought fortune hunters ever higher into the mountains, and in 1860 they began prospecting for gold in the highest valley of the Arkansas River. In April, a tough old character named Abe Lee, after shoveling and sifting tons of frozen gravel, found a few grams of gold in his pans. It was enough to suggest there was sufficient ore in the ground that a mining district could be formed, and in a bit of wishful thinking harking back to the most famous gold rush in history, they named it California Gulch.

Newspapers carried exaggerated stories about news of the strike, and within a few weeks 4,000 had ascended upon the gulch, forever forcing out the Ute Indians who had called the place home. A city—Oro City—sprang up, and along with it came the usual birthing pains of any booming mining camp, from the whiskey-fueled violence to the gamblers and other predators who fed on the honest labors of others.

About this time, Horace Tabor—a twenty-nine-year-old Vermont native who had abandoned his latest failure, a miserably unproductive farm on the Kansas plains—had arrived in the Kansas Territory gold fields, seeking his family's fortune. After a stopover in Denver, he went to Idaho Springs, and then Central City, and finally to the seven-mile-long California Gulch. With his wife and sixteen-month-old son in tow, he staked one of the last claims available, in May 1860.

Mining season at this altitude was six months, from the time the ground thawed and the spring snowmelt put enough water in the rivers and creeks to fill the wooden, hand-shaken sluice boxes, to the time the water stopped flowing in the fall and winter came again. Tons of gravel was shoveled into the sluices, which resulted in buckets of black sand, which then was panned out by hand in the numbingly cold water. The worst of it was the heavy black sand, which nobody could rightly identify, and which hid the gold and made the panning harder than it should have been. But if you were lucky, a day's work would be rewarded by a few grams of gold, or perhaps more. For Horace, there was enough gold in his pans at the end of the day to keep going, and to put a little money aside.

While Horace did the backbreaking work of placer mining, Augusta had a business washing clothes, baking bread, serving meals, selling milk, sorting the mail, and taking in boarders at their little cabin in Oro City.

By January 1861, Kansas had become a state in its own right and relinquished its claim on the gold fields, which were now officially a part of the new Colorado Territory. The Civil War began in April, but it seemed very far away to the miners along the upper Arkansas, waiting for the spring runoff so operations could commence. When mining began, strikes were being pushed ever higher up California Gulch, until gold was not just being teased from the heavy black sand, it was being found as lodes in milky white quartz outcroppings. This gold could be seen, and chipped and hammered away.

During the mining season of 1861, more than a million dollars in gold ore was taken from California Gulch. Many grew rich, but the man who prospered most was Horace Tabor.

Another was Jackson Miles.

"You knew him?" I asked.

"Only too well," she said. "We all knew each other in the gulch, by necessity, but Miles was different. He wasn't calling himself Andrew Jackson Miles yet, but he was a born politician. Sort of like my Horace, but with a mean streak."

"Did Miles have a partner?"

"Yes, for a time," she said. "They both came in the spring of 1860, but by the time Miles announced his strike, the partner was gone."

"Can you remember the partner's name?"

"It was such a long time ago."

"Please, try," I said. "It's important."

While I drained the last of the now-cold tea in my cup, Augusta looked over my shoulder, as if she were trying to read the name on the wall above me. She squinted and rubbed her temple and finally said, "Angus Wright."

I uttered a cry of relief.

"You knew already," she said.

"I suspected, but I needed confirmation."

I opened my valise and took out the list I had copied from the library ledger.

"Look at the name under entry thirteen," I said, handing her the papers. "It is our Angus

Wright. When I confronted Jackson Miles with the name, he claimed to have never heard of the man."

"He's lying," Augusta said.

"But I don't know why."

"Where did you get such a curious list?" Augusta asked.

I told her.

"It is curious that they would note that one of the members was hanged as a horse thief."

"What I find curious are the blank lines scattered about," she said. "Look, they're all primes. Numbers 59 and 61, for example."

"Primes?"

"Numbers that can only be divided, without a remainder, by themselves and one," she said. "All of the blanks are primes, but some of the primes have names, such as number thirteen, Angus Wright."

"What would that mean?"

"I don't know," she said. "But look, Jackson Miles, twenty-three—a prime."

"What about John Shear, the horse thief?"

"Twenty-nine. Prime."

"Prime numbers must have been used to designate a hidden membership within the general membership of the library association," I said. "There was a connection among Miles, Wright, and Shear. Exactly what is unclear, but it must have been something worth keeping secret— and considering Shear's violent death, I'll bet they weren't engaged in charity work."

"Fascinating," Augusta said.

"But why use blank spaces at all?" I asked.

"It's a result of the imperfect ratio of legitimate members to secret ones," she said. "You couldn't expect the pace of the regular membership to exactly match that of those joining for other reasons. As the months wore on, the non-primes filled up quicker than the primes, so you have the last seventeen prime numbers left blank."

"Augusta, you are now approaching sainthood in my eyes."

"Hardly," she said. "It's just schoolgirl math."

"Well, you can keep my books anytime," I said.

"You can't afford me, dear."

"I'm sure I can't. How many primes are there in the first hundred and twenty-five numbers?"

"Thirty," she said.

I again counted the blank spaces.

"There are seventeen blanks, so that gives us thirteen members of this syndicate," I said. "We can assume three—Miles, Wright, and Shear— so that brings the number down to ten."

I tapped the list.

"We are now down to ten names, instead of ninety-nine. The size is becoming manageable."

"Make a new list," Augusta said. "Of the first thirteen primes."

I started with one.

"That's not a prime," she said. "It has to be greater than one."

"So, tell me," I said.

She rattled off the list, and I wrote down the names that went with the numbers:

2.   *A. C. Ford*
3.   *Samuel Blalock*
5.   *Ben Hollister*
7.   *Samuel Drew*
11. *Butch Jones*
17. *Allen Gregory*
19. *Jasper Arnold*
31. *Glen Lewin*
37. *Ethan Smith*
41. *Cade Harland*

"You can draw a line through A. C. Ford," Augusta said. "He was an attorney who was taken from a coach outside Denver and later found shotgunned to death. I clearly remember hearing about it, and reading it in the newspapers, because we were passing through about that time on our way to the gold camps."

"This was about 1860?"

She nodded.

"I should have recognized Shear's name as well, but it's been so long ago. The papers said he was killed by the same group of vigilantes, some sort of secret tribunal."

That's what Patterson, the library association treasurer, had told me as well.

"Do you know what prompted the killings?"

"There had been an epidemic of horse and cattle thefts around Denver City and Auraria, hundreds of animals stolen, and eventually a man was caught in possession of several of the stolen horses," she said. "He was hanged at the head of Cherry Creek, but in an attempt to save his own life, confessed to being part of a vast criminal network. He named the attorney, A. C. Ford, as the boss of the local chapter, and said Shear was his lieutenant. So, there were three executions—two hangings and a buckshot firing squad—within a few days."

"No wonder the library association closed down so quickly," I said. "All of its prime members were being killed. Do you know who any of the members of the vigilance committee may have been?"

"No," she said. "Like I said, we were just passing through."

"Do you remember the name of the first man lynched?"

"He was known by a nickname only, something that sounded Indian. Black Hawk, I think," she said. "That could be any one of the ten persons on the list."

"Yes," I said, "but Black Hawk sounds terribly similar to Blalock, doesn't it? Let's cross Ford off the list, and draw a somewhat lighter line through Blalock. That leaves us with us with eight names. Anybody else on the list ring a bell?"

"Jasper Arnold came here about the time that Miles did. He contracted pneumonia and died that winter."

I crossed Arnold off.

"Seven," I said.

"Do you recognize anyone else?"

She said she didn't.

"What about this Ethan Smith," I said. "I met a Smith in Denver, Eureka Smith, who struck me as exceptionally odd. He was the spirit photographer in the case I told you about. He said he had done some gold prospecting in the past. Do you think Ethan Smith and Eureka Smith may be the same man?"

"I don't remember any Smiths at all," she said. "But there were so many men flowing through the camps at that time. Very much like it is now. They could have been here and I just wouldn't know it. There are still a few old-timers around. I'd go to the saloons—ask for Old Ben Collins, who is one of the originals. Look first at The Great Divide, which is a short walk, to the west end of the gulch. Jackson Miles built The Divide so fast after striking it rich they say some of the walls were built from packing crates."

26

By the light of a lamp on the nightstand, I lay in bed and went over my notes. With Augusta's help, I had made tremendous progress, but there was still more to puzzle out.

There was a hand mirror on the nightstand, glass up, and I could see Horrible Hank's green face as he tried to turn his head to the correct angle to get a peek in my direction.

"Enough of that," I said, reaching out to turn the mirror over.

"Don't flatter yourself," Hank said. "You bored me silly long ago. I'm trying to see the sketch on the back of that paper. Is that a drawing of a hitch?"

"It's something I made so I wouldn't forget what the knot used in poor Charlie Howart's suspension looked like," I said. "It had to be untied to get him down."

"Why didn't you just cut the rope?"

"Because the knot would still be attached to the leg of the stove," I said. "Why are you asking?"

"It's a common hitch, used to secure steamboats to docks," he said.

"Something nautical, then?"

"Yes, a Lighterman's hitch, or a variation."

I picked up the mirror and held it over the drawing.

"You're certain?"

"Who's the steamboater here?"

"Would it be used on vessels other than steamboats?"

"Certainly," he said. "Mean something?" he asked.

"Maybe," I said.

"Oh, there's one other thing," Hank said. "I was lying when I said you bored me. How about showing a little shoulder, seeing as how we're all cozy in bed?"

"You're impossible," I said. "Why don't you just go away?"

I turned the mirror facedown on the nightstand.

The jolting of the train as it slows and then eases forward again brings me fully asleep. I sit up and look out the windows of the car, and see that we are pulling into a brightly lit station in the middle of a great city.

The car is empty, except for the old man and me.

"Where are we?" I ask.

The old man beside me shakes his head.

"You still don't know anything."

"Why are you so rude?"

"Because I'm forgotten," he says.

The train stops and I can see people standing patiently on the platform, men and women of all ages, and children, but they each stand apart from one another, so it does not seem that any of them constitute a family. They begin filing into the train.

I go forward and find the conductor, who is taking tickets from the new passengers, punching them, and handing them back. The tickets are yellow and blue and green. They all say, "COFFIN TICKET—WATERLOO TO BROOKWOOD—LONDON NECROPOLIS RAILWAY," and each ticket has a unique ten-digit number in small type.

"It doesn't matter where you sit," the conductor keeps telling the new passengers. "There's no class division here, you've left all that behind. Sit wherever you like."

"Where are we?" I ask, struggling against the flood of new arrivals.

"Cemetery Station," the conductor says. "London."

"How did we get to England?" I ask. "Trains can't cross the ocean."

"You'll have to take all matters of physics up with the superintendent."

"If I'm asleep, then how can I read what's written on the tickets?" I ask. "I can only read numbers when I'm dreaming, not words."

"You're not exactly asleep, are you?" he asks.

"This is a part of Waterloo Station, then?" I ask. "A real place? Not a dream place, not something found in a storybook or told to children to make them behave?"

"Cemetery Station is very real."

"And what is Brookwood?"

"Brookwood is the final destination," he says. "Brookwood Cemetery is a lovely, restful place, made just for the Necropolis Railway. It's only a forty-five-minute ride away."

"What are you saying?"

"The superintendent explained it to you already."

"That I can either go mad or choose to get off at the final destination?"

"That would be your choice."

"To hell with this," I say. "You go to the end of the line without me. I'm stepping off here."

I brush past the conductor and the line of newly dead, and reach the door of the car. I expect that I will somehow be prevented from reaching the platform—there will be an invisible force to throw me back, or I will find myself back in the car with the old man, or I will just go to wake—but nothing happens when I leave the car. I walk a few steps and turn around and look at the train, with its curious green engine and its squat cars, and the caskets being hauled into the coffin car by the scampering widdershins.

I turn and walk away.

I find a broad set of metal stairs leading down, away from the raised platforms of Cemetery Station. When I reach the base of the stairs, I find myself in the cavernous central part of the station, the largest building I have ever seen, all metal and stone and huge windows and skylights and bustling with life. There are living people waiting to board trains, and leaving trains, and buying newspapers and eating snacks, and rushing to do all of the things that living people are accustomed to do. And the sound—it is extraordinary, a symphony of chatter and footsteps and hissing, actual trains.

Laughing with joy, I rush to a family who is about to ascend a platform for a departure.

"Please, help me get back home," I say. "If only you could lend me a little money, so that I could send a transatlantic wire asking for help, or if that's too much to ask, if I could just get directions to the American embassy."

They don't seem to hear me. Not the mother, father, or three children.

"Listen to me," I say. "I need your help."

There is no response.

"How rude!" I bark.

I rush to a man reading a newspaper while getting his shoes shined.

"I urgently need a moment of your time," I say. "You see, I'm from America—you could have guessed that from my accent—and through no fault of my own, I've become stranded here. Spirited away, as it were. I don't even know what part of London the station is in, so if you could just give me some direction on how to find any other group of Americans, or even the London bureau of the Herald-Tribune, *I would be eternally grateful."*

Neither the man nor the bootblack act as if they hear me.

Infuriated, I reach out to snatch the newspaper that is hiding the man's face, but watch in horror as my hand passes through the paper—and I feel nothing.

I rush to a dozen more people, one at a time, shout-

ing and waving my arms, even stamping my feet, but my antics have no effect.

It isn't just that I am invisible.

I have become a ghost.

My unfinished business is back up the metal stairway, at the Cemetery Station, and it is getting ready to pull away. I imagine spending an eternity in Waterloo Station, shouting and waving my arms at people who can neither see nor hear me.

I run back to the stairs as fast as I can.

27

There was one thing that set The Great Divide apart from all other saloons in the Leadville district, and probably every saloon in the state of Colorado, Denver included: the twenty-foot-long diamond dust mirror behind the bar.

The Divide was built hard against a slope at the end of California Gulch, and looked as if it were three or four buildings nailed together. There was the main room of the saloon itself, which was the oldest part of the building, but over the years additions had been tacked on: a second floor that had a balcony, a separate wing that housed a restaurant, even a cupola with a wrought-iron eagle clutching an iron ball at the top. And all of it was painted firehouse red.

It was a saloon designed by a madman.

I had come to The Divide early, not yet nine o'clock, hoping to catch some talkative old-timers before the place became packed with thirsty miners. The door to the saloon was open, and the mirror caught the morning sun and bathed the interior with warm light. Already there were a dozen men scattered about the place, drinking silently.

The interior of the place was as weird as the exterior. The mirror was its most famous feature, but the walls had the wildest collection of objects I'd ever seen assembled in one place. It was a museum to eccentricity, including an entire menagerie of stuffed animals known to be lethal to humans, from a diamondback rattlesnake to a grizzly bear. There were dressmaker forms draped with unfinished calicos, a pair of rusting last stands from a long-closed cobbler's shop, and a white porcelain head that had its bumps segregated by dotted lines into aspects of personality and character *(religiosity, friendship, combativeness)*.

But the thing that made me most uncomfortable was the collections of human teeth, in huge frames with inked descriptions *(mandibular first molar)* from defunct medical schools *(Beitzinger College of Dentistry, Topeka)*.

As I walked up to the bar, I tried to ignore Hank, who was floating in the mirror like a bather in a swimming pool.

"How grand," he exclaimed. "Finally, room to breathe!"

I shook my head at him.

"I'm here on business," I said. "Can't you be quiet for once?"

Hank stuck his tongue out at me.

"Beg your pardon, miss?" the bartender said.

"Talking to myself," I said. "Bad habit."

"What can I get you?"

The bartender placed his palms on the bar and leaned forward, obviously relieving the stress on his back. He had blue eyes and a ruddy complexion and his accent was Irish Bronx.

"Do you know," I asked, "are any of the gentleman drinking in the back, would they be old-timers who were around fifteen or eighteen years ago?"

"No," the bartender said. "They're recent, like most of us."

"Too bad," I said.

"What are you drinking?"

"Something light."

"You mean like rum or gin?"

"Lighter."

"Beer?"

"Something without alcohol," I said.

He cocked his head.

"Not much call for anything that don't have a kick," he said.

I asked for water. He nodded, then went to the end of the bar and filled a glass from a pitcher. He came back and placed the glass in front of me with as much gravity as if it were a double whiskey.

"Thanks," I said. "Nice mirror."

"Diamond dust," he said.

"Must be worth a fortune."

"It cost a fortune to get here, but it's not made of diamonds," he said. "All mirrors are backed with silver, but diamond dust mirrors have quicksilver added to them so that it spreads over the glass evenly."

"Almost like a photographic plate."

"I suppose," the bartender said. "If you look closely, there's a fine grain to the backing, which resembles diamond dust."

"It is beautiful," I said. "How did they ever get it up here?"

"Andrew Jackson Miles paid for it, that's how," he said. "He built the place and he had this mirror shipped in special from St. Louis. Can you imagine it surviving the trip in a freight wagon all the way from the depot in Canon City?"

"Can you imagine how much bad luck there would be if you broke *that* mirror?" I asked. "Instead of seven years, it might be seven hundred."

The bartender laughed.

"Everybody is scared to go near it," he said. "It gives me the fantods just to polish it. Can you imagine having to tell Mister Miles that you broke his mirror? No, thanks."

"Do you know Jackson Miles?"

"Sure, I know Jacks," he said. "He hired me."

"When was that?"

"A year, maybe longer," he said.

"He built this place after he struck it rich?"

"The first time," he said. "Both Jacks and old man Tabor made plenty of money from California Gulch, but it was the silver that made them as rich as Solomon. The gold rush didn't last but a couple of years. Sixty-two, I think, was the last year it came close to producing a million dollars.

After that, the decline was pretty steady. The Tabors stayed, but Jacks lit out for Denver—but he kept control of his saloon and his claims here. They weren't making much money, but he said he kept them for sentimental reasons."

"So when was the silver discovered?"

"In 1876—same year Colorado became a state— somebody figured out the heavy black sand that had been clogging the gold sluices was really a mixture of lead and silver. They knew about the lead already, but the concentration of silver was a surprise—a hundred ounces per ton."

"They had been throwing away fortunes," I said.

"Exactly. And because silver was way up over one dollar per ounce, it didn't take much ciphering to know that a person could get wealthy fast. The mining moved from the gulch north to Leadville, and Jacks was first to strike it rich, because he had the means necessary to get the silver out of the ground first. Tabor got richer, too, but Jacks was first."

"Sounds like his success is made of a little luck and a whole lot of ambition."

"That's why he'll be the next governor of the state," the bartender said. "And that's why I'll tend bar for the rest of my life, and with this aching back of mine."

"What happened?"

"Had a Burleigh fall from a column jack and pin me under it," he said. "It didn't break my back, but it cracked it. I was a damned good drill operator, at least until I got hurt. And when you get hurt, you're on your own. Nobody wanted to hire a half-crippled Mick with a bad attitude."

All the while the poor bartender was talking about getting hurt by the drill, Hank was rolling his eyes. He had placed himself in such a way that it appeared, at least to my eyes, that he was sitting on the bar stool next to me.

"That's nothing," Hank said. "He should be in a steamboat explosion and be mortally scalded by the steam. Now, *that's* some pain."

"Tell me about the drilling," I said, trying not to look in the mirror.

The bartender gave me a brief history of the Burleigh compressed air automatic drill, and the heavier steam-powered drill that came before it, and how he had come from New York with nothing but the clothes on his back and had learned mining from the ground up. In Nevada, he had started as a nipper—somebody who carries tools and replacement parts down to the drillers—then began as a driller's helper, and finally came to Colorado as a fully fledged operator.

"You were working for the Miles operation?"

"Another consolidated, the Empire," he said. "But Jacks heard about the accident and gave me a job here. He said my primary duty is to protect that mirror. So, if a drunk gets the least bit rowdy—he's out of here. Not going to chance any poorly aimed bottles breaking it."

"Didn't know Miles had a soft streak."

"He does," the bartender said. "Take this place, for instance. We're at one end of California

Gulch, or what used to be the gulch before they blasted and washed it away. A normal person would have moved this place to Leadville, where the business is. But Jackson wanted to keep it here, because it was the site of one of his early gold claims."

"You mean, over the shaft?"

"Well, it was more of a drift than a shaft."

"A drift?"

"A horizontal tunnel into the rock. The building is built against a huge rock face with a quartz outcropping where a rich lode was found. Jacks sent a declined drift into it. It's behind us, somewhere."

"Why didn't he mine it for silver?"

"No silver in quartz," the bartender said, putting his hands on his hips and stretching backward for his back. "And I think Jacks just wanted to seal up the claim and keep it as it was, for sentimental reasons. He knew the silver rush would destroy everything that stood in its way."

"From what I've seen," I said, "he may be right."

"Jacks is very fond of this place," the bartender said. "He stops by, every other month or so, and when he does he brings some of the stuff you see on the walls. He's got a sense of humor, he does."

"This place is a monument to fatal, failed, and unfinished business."

"I don't see that," the bartender said, shrugging.

He put a jar of pickled eggs and a bowl of fruit on the bar.

"No sandwiches yet," he said. "Not until lunchtime."

"Thanks," I said, taking an apple. "What do I owe you?"

"On the house," he said. He wiped his right hand on the towel thrown across his shoulder and held it out.

We shook.

"I'm Francis Gallagher," he said.

"Pleased to meet you, Frank."

I gave him my real name. If Jacks wanted to know who had been asking questions, there was no point hiding behind something fake.

"You in camp on some kind of business?" he asked.

"An inquiry," I said.

"Do you have an interest in a mine?" he asked.

"You might say that."

"That's why you were asking about the old-timers," he said. "It must be some business that goes way back."

"Something I inherited."

I still hadn't taken a bite of the apple, so I put it into my jacket pocket.

"If you're looking for information on one of the old claims," he said, "you might go on down to old Oro City. It's only two and a half miles east of here, around the base of Carbonate Hill. There's still a few buildings and the old hotel there."

"Thanks, Frank," I said, and stepped down from the stool.

"Come back if you have the time."

I promised I would, and started for the door. Frank smiled, then left the bar to attend to some business in the next room.

"Hey!" Hank shouted.

"What is it now?" I whispered over my shoulder.

"I need some help," he said.

I turned.

"What kind of help?"

"There's something about this mirror," he said. "I'm stuck."

"Stuck?"

"I can't get out," he said. "I'm trying to follow you, but I can't. The mirror is different than others. This diamond dust or quicksilver or whatever it's called has captured me like a photograph."

I thought about that for about two seconds.

"Farewell, Hank. Good luck finding somebody else to torture."

28

The walk to Oro City was pleasant, even though I had to thread my way through a maze of claims and mine workings. Not only were there the new operations to walk through or around, but the remains of the frenzy that had taken place sixteen or eighteen years before, including a rotting wooden aqueduct that had diverted the Arkansas River, miles away to the west, to fill the sluice boxes of California Gulch.

Even though it was the second of July, the weather was cool and pleasant. It felt good to walk, after having spent so much time in courtrooms and stage coaches and strange beds during the past week. It took me less than thirty minutes to reach Oro City, which was well on its way to becoming a ghost town. There were a handful of weather-beaten structures clustered at the base of a red-tinged slope called Iron Hill, and some of them had already been deserted. The grocery and the old hotel were still open for business, however. The hotel was an unpainted, two-story structure with a large porch, and on the porch there was a white-haired old man sitting in a ratty cane chair. The man was smoking a cigarette he'd rolled from a bag of fixing that hung from the pocket of his blue plaid shirt.

"How do you do," I said.

"I get by," he said. "Some days better than others."

"Mind if I sit with you?"

"You'll have to get your own chair."

"I don't need a chair."

I scooted onto the porch deck, with my back against a post, facing the old man. He smoked and stared at me beneath bushy white eyebrows, and after a few minutes he finally spoke.

"We had a few women in the old days who dressed in men's clothes," he said. "Not fancy suit clothes like yours, but work clothes. They did the work, too, and most of them could best any man in camp. We didn't have many of them, but we had a few. Are you like that?"

"I'm not much of a fighter."

"You must be here sniffing around a claim."

"Nope," I said. "I'm looking for somebody, an old-timer like you. Ben Collins. I was told he was an original."

"Who told you that?"

"Augusta Tabor."

The old man laughed.

"Augusta," he said. "That sounds like her. How's she doing?"

"She and Horace are doing well," I said. "Better than that, even. She told me he wants to build an opera house in Leadville."

The old man shook his head.

"That's crazy."

"Are you the original Ben?"

"Maybe," he said. "What do you want if I am?"

"I'm trying to solve a puzzle," I said. "And to do it, I need some information about people who were here, and in Denver, going back eighteen years ago."

"You're talking about a lot of people."

"Yes, but I have just seven names I'm interested in."

I pulled the list from my pocket and offered it to him.

"I can't read it, girl," he said. "My close vision went years ago."

"All right," I said. "I can read it to you."

I read the first three names—Ben Hollister, Samuel Drew, Butch Jones—and his face darkened so that I stopped.

"What is the matter?" I asked.

It took him a minute to answer.

"Read the other names."

"Allen Gregory, Glen Lewin, Ethan Smith, and Cade Harland."

The old man dropped the cigarette on the porch and ground it out beneath his heel. Then he leaned forward, his yellow eyes staring toward the peaks to the southwest.

"That's Mount Elbert there," he said, pointing

at the tallest one. "It's fourteen thousand and four hundred and some odd feet tall, the highest peak in all of the Rocky Mountains. Ain't none higher, not any of the peaks of the whole damn range, from New Mexico Territory to British Columbia. That's something, isn't it?"

I stared at the mountain, which looked like a squat pyramid amid a row of other squat pyramids. Their summit was a squat gray pyramid marbled with snow.

"It's beautiful," I said.

"It's so damned high that nobody reached the top, at least not until the Hayden Survey came four years ago. I wish to hell they hadn't. We ruin everything we touch. Do you know who Mount Elbert is named for?"

I said I didn't.

"Sam Elbert, the territorial governor, who made a treaty with the Utes that opened up three million acres of their reservation to mining and railroading. Three million acres. And look what we've done to it. We spoil every damned thing we touch."

"Like I said, I'm not here about a claim."

"I know why you're here," he said. "I've been waiting for you, or somebody like you, for a long time. I'm tired, and I'm dying. Cancer is eating me up. It's down deep in my guts. I was afraid that I'd die before somebody came and asked the question."

"Then you'll help me, Mister Collins?"

"I'm not Collins," he said.

I told him I didn't understand.

"I'm not Ben Collins," he repeated. "My real name is Ben Hollister, the first name you read on your list. And I'm going to help you to keep Jackson Miles from becoming another one of these sons of bitches who gets their names put on mountains."

29

Over the next two hours, Ben Hollister told me how he'd been part of the horse and cattle theft gang in Denver City. There was no vast syndicate, he said, just an odd group of characters who had met at the Elephant Corral and decided to take systematic advantage of the amount of traffic passing through Denver to get to the Kansas Territory gold fields. Hollister said he was nearing forty at the time and was the oldest member of the gang, but had the most experience as a horse thief, having learned the trade in the Indian Nations on the other side of the river from Fort Smith, Arkansas.

A. C. Ford was an attorney who specialized in representing the lower elements of Denver society, and as the only educated member of the gang and, handily, secretary of the library association, it had been his idea to use the membership as a cover. Orders were conveyed by means of a book cipher. Messages consisted of a long list of numbers that would mean nothing unless the reader knew that the numbers stood for words in a book (24,10 would mean the tenth word of the twenty-fourth page, for example) and, more importantly, knew which book was used to encode the message. Because the names of the gang members were unlikely to all appear in any text, they were referred to by their prime numbers from the library ledger. A. C. Ford had a personal copy of the book used for encoding messages, and the library association had the other—W. L. Gresham's *Syrinx of the Seven Worlds.*

But things fell apart when Samuel Blalock was nabbed by the local vigilance committee in possession of stolen horses and, in bargaining for his life, named Ford as the leader of the gang and Shear as lieutenant. If the committee had been more patient, they might have unraveled the mystery of the other gang members, but their buckshot and rope put an end to further inquiry.

The surviving gang members fled Denver.

Young Jackson Miles and Angus Wright wound up at California Gulch, as did Ben Hollister, while the others were scattered from Idaho Springs to Buckskin Joe.

"Are you prepared to testify to all of this?"

"If I live long enough," he said.

"You've seen a doctor."

He waved his hand.

"I saw a doctor. He didn't tell my anything I didn't know already."

"We'll get a notary here tomorrow," I said. "Just in case . . ."

He nodded.

"There's more I want to tell," he said. "What happened in Denver—it wasn't just stealing. There was worse, hired murders even, all ordered through those slips with those damn rows of numbers. I'll swear to it."

"Didn't happen to keep any of those secret orders, did you?"

"Burned them," he said. "All of them. Except for one. Kept it to remind myself of my wickedness."

"Where is it?"

A shaking hand went to the pocket where the muslin Durham sack hung. His brought out a folded paper yellow with age and brown with sweat, and handed it to me.

"I told you, I've been waiting for you to come. I've been ready."

I unfolded the paper.

It contained several rows of two- and three-digit numbers, joined by commas, all written in ink in a careful hand. There were two numbers in the rows not joined by commas, the primes 5 and 23.

"That's an order for Jackson Miles and me to steal the cayuses of some pilgrims just arrived in Auraria City," he said. "Look the numbers up in the red book and that's what it will tell you. That Andrew Jackson Miles is a horse thief."

"Let me keep this, won't you?"

I folded the paper and slipped it into my jacket pocket.

"Tell me what happened between Angus Wright and Jackson Miles."

Hollister shrugged.

"Wright just disappeared one day," he said. "Jackson said he had come to him the night before and said he'd had enough, that the work was too hard and he was ready to move on. Jackson said he agreed to buy his claim—"

"They weren't partners?"

"No," Hollister said. "They each had their own operation. A couple of days after Jackson took possession of the mine—The Great Divide—he struck one of the richest gold quartz veins in the district."

"Convenient," I said. "Who had the red book last?"

"Ethan Smith went to the library and got it before he quit town," Hollister said. "Don't know what became of Ford's copy of the book, but we didn't care, because if they found it—so what? Nobody could link that book to us with the ledger with the key to the names. Don't know what happened to Smith after that. Changed his name, probably."

"To Charlie Howart," I said. "Ended up in Kansas."

"How is he?"

"Hanged," I said. "Last week."

"Not surprised," Hollister said. "I reckon Jackson

Miles couldn't let anybody live who knew any part of the real story."

"Any idea who killed him?" I asked.

"I haven't been off this porch in a month," he said.

"What happened to my other names on the list?"

"Drew and Jones quit Colorado and were killed holding up a bank in Utah," he said. "Gregory died of fever, the first winter in the camp. Glen Lewin blew his brains out over a woman."

"That just leaves Cade Harland," I said.

"Harland," he said. "That kid was the worst of the lot."

"Tell me," I said.

"I'm tired," Hollister said. "And thirsty."

"I'll get you some water."

"The hell with that. Whiskey."

I went into the hotel and asked if there were a notary in Oro City. The sad woman behind the desk said no, but that Leadville was crawling with them. She asked me if I wanted a room, and I said no, but that I needed a glass of water and a shot of whisky for the old man on the porch.

"Old man Collins?" she asked. "Sure, I keep a bottle for him."

"Does he have any family that you know of?"

"Nobody ever comes to visit him," she said. "No letters, either. He's sick, you know. The cancer."

"I know."

"He used to go into Leadville and drink at The

Great Divide, but it's been months since he could make the trip," she said. "Poor thing."

I paid and took the whiskey and the water to the porch.

The old man was slumped over in the cane chair.

"No," I said. "Oh, no."

I put the glasses down and knelt beside him. The front of his shirt and the bag of cigarette makings were covered with his blood, and it puddled beneath the ratty cane chair. Confused, I gently tugged his head upright—and discovered that somebody had slit the old man's throat.

30

Whoever had killed the old man couldn't be far away. I looked up and down the street, but nobody stood out as suspicious—there was nobody running, or glancing over their shoulder, or with blood on their clothes. It was just business as usual, from the man loading a wagon with bits of discarded lumber to the woman who carried her laundry on one hip and a crying baby on the other.

Then I thought—the killer was probably watching me right now.

I went back inside the hotel and asked the sad woman to summon the sheriff and the undertaker. She asked who would pay for the funeral, but she didn't ask how the old man had died.

I gave her a twenty-dollar note, then left by the back door.

The killer was probably watching the front of the hotel, waiting for me to leave so he could follow. Or, he was waiting somewhere along the road back to Leadville, his knife at the ready.

I didn't wait in the hotel because it might take a half an hour for either the law or the undertaker to arrive, and I didn't want to be waiting alone with the sad woman. It would be nothing for the killer to slip in and kill both of us in a matter of moments. No, I wanted to get away unseen.

From the back of the hotel, I ran in the direction of Mount Elbert, generally southwest, not really knowing where I was going, but intent on turning back north to Leadville and the safety of Tabor's store.

Driven by fear, I positively flew through the old mining district. I didn't slow down until I reached a steep hillside studded with pine trees. My shoes slid in the loose rock and my legs went out from under me and I fell, then rolled and came hard up against a cedar stump. I wasn't hurt badly, just bruised, but the horror of the old man's murder—and the loss of my key witness—crashed down on me.

I cursed, in English, and then I cried.

What was I going to do now, I asked myself. I was 500 miles from home, in the roughest mining camp in America, having made a mortal enemy of the man destined to be the next governor of Colorado, and was on the run from a killer—and I was alone.

I felt sorry for myself for perhaps five minutes.

Then I picked myself up, brushed the dirt from my clothes, and made my way down the hillside. I tried to go north, but an impossibly steep ridge prevented it, so I continued down. I continued hopelessly lost for the next hour or so, until finally I could hear the rush of water—and I knew if I followed the river upstream it would lead me back toward Leadville.

The river was twenty or thirty feet across, with gravel banks and strewn with boulders. The going along the riverbank was just as hard as making my way through the pine forest. I was panting from exertion, and my clothes had become damp with sweat, so I stopped and peeled off my coat.

I folded it and placed it on a flat rock.

The rock overlooked a short section of curling and hissing rapids. It was comforting, and somewhat hypnotic, to stare at the rushing green water. This, I thought, is what the Arkansas River must have looked like before—well, before we got to it. I sat down on the rock, resting.

But the rapids made so much noise that I didn't hear the Sky Pilot approaching me from upstream—and I didn't even know he was behind me until he shouted, nearly in my ear.

"Sister!"

I sprang from the rock.

"Stay away from me," I said.

He stepped forward, his right hand outstretched.

"I know who you are," I said, backing away. "Your name is Cade Harland, and you killed the old man and I told everybody in Oro City that you did it, so it's no good killing me, because your secret is out."

"We're all sinners," he said, still advancing.

I turned to make a run for it but tripped on one of the millions of blasted rocks that lined the river bank.

The Sky Pilot was on me in a moment, and his right hand closed around my wrist like a band of stone. Then he began dragging me across a gravel bar to an eddy, a pool of still water above the rapids. He had only one hand around me—the other held the Bible aloft—and I was fighting and kicking with all three of my free limbs, but it was no good. He was just too strong.

"Rock of Ages, cleft for thee," he sang. "Let me hide myself in thee."

He waded out into the swift water, pulling me with him.

I pleaded with him.

"Please," I said. "I won't say anything. I'll do anything you want. . . ."

"Don't fight it, sister," he said.

We were thigh-deep in the water now, and it was cold, and I could feel the pressure of the current piling against my legs. He released my wrist, just for a moment, just long enough to get a grip on the front of my vest.

"Do you believe, sister?"

We were face-to-face, the Sky Pilot standing over me.

"Oh, God!" I cried.

"I baptize you in the name of the Father, the Son, and the Holy Ghost!"

He pushed me down into the water.

I saw the sky and the mountains and trees disappear and be replaced with a cloud of my own red hair in the swirling bluish green water. The water against my face was cold, shockingly cold, like nothing I had ever felt before. I could hear the hollow rush of the water and the clink of stones as they moved along the bottom. And there was something else—the soft murmur of voices.

I fought with both hands against his wrist, but I had even poorer leverage now than I did on the bank.

The sound of the voices was stronger now, and they were all the voices of all of those who had died in the river since the beginning of time, an untold number of drownings and killings and suicides, all the way down to the confluence of the Mississippi.

The bluish green light above me began to wink and go dim.

The voices were stronger, gasping and struggling and pleading.

"No!" the chorus screamed.

I could feel my heels skitter along the bed of the river; feel my shirttail loose and billowing in the current; feel the icy embrace of the river as it coursed down my back and along my sides and between my legs.

"No! No! No!"

And then I realized it was me who was screaming the word, the sound made weird by the water, the meaning rendered useless by the intent of the hulking figure holding me under.

I had used the last of my air to shout, over and over, a cry of protest.

Then bloody raindrops began to sprinkle the water. They fell and bloomed and streaked downstream. For a moment I thought I was dreaming again, until the burning in my lungs convinced me otherwise.

I wanted to breathe, but I forced myself not to.

The river went dark and soon even the sound of the water began to grow faint. Then everything went dark, except for a single point of light that floated just above me. It was a tiny ball of white light, hard and brilliant.

My body screamed for me to take a breath.

I fixed my attention on the light. There was the light, and nothing else.

Then I was jerked up and out of the water and back into the world.

I took great gulps of air.

The Sky Pilot held me yet, grinning madly, the Bible still in one hand. But the water around us was crimson with blood. At first I thought it was my blood, but then I saw the wound to the side of his face, a gunshot that had carried away his left ear and much of the side of his head.

The Bible fell into the water and floated downstream.

The preacher released me, and I half swam and half clawed my way to the gravel bar. I rolled over onto my back, wheezing and coughing up what seemed like half of the Arkansas River.

"Jack!" I shouted, trying to get the hair out of

my eyes so I could see. It had to be Calder. McCarty must have told him I'd gone to Denver, I thought, and he had tracked me down from there.

I sat up and saw the preacher on the gravel bank, ten yards away, facedown. The blood dripped from the side of his head into the water, carried away like red ribbons in the current.

"Jack," I said again, turning around.

"Calling for your partner?"

An English accent.

It was Chatwin, the mudlark. He was standing twenty yards behind me, a revolver in his hand, the satchel over his shoulder, and the briar pipe in his mouth. The breeze was bringing the smell of the pipe tobacco in my direction, and it seemed discordant with the scene that had just played out.

"Calder's not here, I'm afraid."

"But you," I said.

"I told you I was going to Leadville. And lo, here I am."

"You saved my life," I said, the phrases coming out in spurts. "I thought I would drown. I was in the water such a long time. And you shot Cade Harland. He killed Howart and also the old man at Oro City."

Chatwin walked down the bank, his boots crunching on the gravel. Then he turned and sat on his kneels next to me, holding the nasty little revolver up over his right shoulder, so the barrel lay behind his neck.

Where I couldn't reach it.

"You have it all wrong," the mudlark said. "The preacher was nobody. I wasn't trying to save your life. I was aiming at you and hit the lunatic instead."

He paused.

"I'm Cade Harland."

"Oh, no," I said, burrowing the back of my head into the gravel. "The old man, Hollister. He had called Cade Harland the kid. I had just thought it was a gang nickname."

"No, I really was a child," he said. "Barely in my teens."

I thought of the boys in Leadville, the ones who had delighted in kicking the preacher.

"Where did you get the gun?" I asked.

"I carry it in the satchel," he said. "It's a handy little thing, a .44-caliber Belgian-made British Bulldog. I had it when we spoke on the bank of the river at Dodge City, when I said that I was disarmed by your beauty. Alas, you were right— I was merely distracted. If I had known what trouble you would make, I would have killed you then."

"Feeling's mutual," I said.

"I heard everything, from around the corner of the porch," he said. "I had to kill him, before he identified me, before you could get a sworn statement from him. When you went inside for a few minutes, it gave me enough time to come up behind him and do the job. If anybody saw it, they would have thought nothing of it—just a friend with his arm around an old man, leaning close, offering a bit of comfort."

"And to think," I said, "I had made up my mind to allow you into my bed if I ever saw you again. But now I'm reconsidering that decision, because everything you told me was a lie."

"Oh, no," he said. "It was all the truth, except about my name and serving in the place of a rich man's son and then deserting. Instead, I came west as soon as I reached America, and joined with Jackson Miles and his gang in 1860. I couldn't really tell you the truth about that, could I?"

"But why did you tell me you were coming here?"

"I thought things might lead you here," he said. "So I told you that so you wouldn't be suspicious if we ran into each other here. It would make it easier, you know."

"To kill me."

"But you've made things very hard indeed," he said. "I didn't count on having to kill the old man before he died of cancer, or chase you down to the river here. But it's fitting in a way. This is where we met—on the banks of the same river."

"So you're going to kill me here."

"Of course, but I'm not going to leave your body here, because it would cause an inquiry. Nobody cares about the crazy preacher—nobody even knows his name—but you, you've already made friends with Augusta Tabor, and you've told everyone you've met that you're investigating Jackson Miles. I can't just leave your body here on the gravel bar."

I began to shiver.

"I'm going to haul your body over this bloody rock garden called Colorado and drop your body down one of the old shafts on the hillside behind us, so nobody will ever find you. Just like Angus Wright."

"You killed him for Jacks."

"He didn't have the stones for it, but I did," Cade said. "Old Angus found the bonanza, and Jacks wanted it. I chained him up to a bloody huge slab of rock in the Great Divide mine and left him there. Then Jacks built the saloon on the spot, to seal off the drift where I'd left Angus. He's added to The Divide over the years, made it fancier with that mirror and such, but it is still a monument to greed and murder."

"His greed," I said. "Your killing. A partnership in murder."

"Don't let anybody tell you crime doesn't pay," Cade said. "It pays bloody well, and keeps on paying. Jacks has made more money off the silver boom than he did on the gold—and it was old Angus Wright's gold that made him rich in the first place."

"You've done all of his killing for him, from the beginning," I said. "You killed Charlie Howart, didn't you? Made it look like a suicide. You must have had some conversation with him first, and he may have told you about the haunting, so hanging him over the rafter would seem appropriate. But you didn't find the book, did you?"

"Not so bad," he said. "You might make a good

detective after all, if you only had another two or three lifetimes of mistakes to make. Tell me, where was the book?"

"The kindling box had a false bottom."

"Ah," he said.

"Do you still take your orders from Jacks via coded messages?"

He shook his head.

"No need," he said. "I anticipate what he needs and take care of it."

"Like killing me," I said.

I crossed my arms and hugged my own chest.

"You're scared."

"I'm shaking because I'm cold," I said.

"No shame," he said. "The fear of death is quite natural. Why, I've seen grown men shake like lambs when their time had come."

"My only consolation," I said, "is that Jackson Miles will eventually hire someone to kill you, too. He has to. Once I'm gone, you're the only thing left connecting him to any of this."

"Jacks doesn't have the stones."

"No, but he'll get somebody who does to do it for him," I said.

"Now, isn't this where you say it would be better for me to go to the coppers? That I'm only safe if Jacks is in prison, or hanged?"

"You already know that."

"Then this is where you beg."

"Va au diable," I spat. *Go to hell.*

"You first, love. Now, turn over."

"Why?"

He put the gun in the satchel and tossed it out of reach. Then he pulled a knife from his boot, a knife with a six-inch blade that was crusty with the old man's dried blood.

"I told you, turn over, onto your stomach," he said. "I don't want to look at your face when I cut your throat."

"No."

He hit me in the face. Hard.

I fought back, trying to kick and claw my way free. He climbed on top of me and pinned my upper arms with his knees. He grabbed my hair with his left hand and jerked my head back, exposing my neck.

Then he placed the cold blade of the knife to my throat.

"Have it your way," he said. "It makes it easier for me."

Then he pushed a little harder with the knife, and it was so sharp I didn't feel the cut, but I did feel the warm trickle of blood spilling down my neck. Then he got an odd look in his eyes and eased the pressure on the blade.

"You know, you're right about one thing," he said, leaning so close I could smell the tobacco on his breath. "If I didn't have to kill you quick to save my boss's political career, I would fancy having a go—"

He didn't get to finish the thought, because a great rock came smashing down on the top of his head. His eyes went unfocused and his mouth went slack, but he did not drop the knife. Then the rock came again, a sideways blow to the temple, and Cade gave a small cry and the blade slipped from his fingers and he toppled over, falling unmoving on the ground.

I snatched up the knife and threw it in the water.

The Sky Pilot stood over me with the bloody rock in his left hand.

The right side of his body seemed to droop, his right arm was limp, and his right foot was turned at an unnatural angle. The gunshot to the left side of his head was wet with blood and flecked with bone and little bits that may have been brain tissue.

The preacher looked at Cade, and he looked at me, and then he let the rock drop to the ground. He nodded, as if acknowledging I was safe; then he sat on the gravel bar and stared at the river.

"Jordan," he said, slurring the word badly.

"Yes," I said. "Jordan."

"Say it."

"Say what?" I asked.

He tried to make a sentence, and although I heard only two words, "a comfort," I understood.

He slumped over and I pulled his head into my lap. He was still wearing the green kerchief I had loaned to him in Dodge City, but it was now caked with blood.

"'Take no thought for your life,'" I recited. "'Consider the ravens: for they neither sow nor reap; which neither have storehouse nor barn; and God feedeth them: how much more are ye better than the fowls?'"

"Amen," the Sky Pilot said.

And there he died.

31

My jacket still lay folded on the flat rock. The garment still had my notes and the cipher that Hollister had given me tucked safely into the pocket. It was also dry, so I threw it over my shoulders, because I was shivering from the cold. Then I felt the apple, the one the bartender had given me at The Great Divide, and was grateful to have a little something to eat.

After I finished the apple, I went over to Cade's body and kicked it, to make sure he was truly dead. He didn't move, but I wasn't convinced. So I may have picked up a rock and struck him in the head one or three times more, just to make sure.

Then I slung the satchel over my shoulder, the one with the ugly British Bulldog revolver, and set out in the direction of Leadville. It was late in the afternoon now, and I did not want to spend the night on the river bank with two dead men.

My shoes were wet and my feet soon began to

hurt, and as the sun got lower in the sky it became colder right quick. But in less than a mile I came to a bend where I could see a coach road close to the west side of the river, and eventually I found a shallow place to cross by hopping from one boulder to the next. I fought my way through a willow tree, then scrambled up the bank to the road.

Before long, there was a coach. It was going at breakneck speed, all flying hooves and spinning wheels, and it must have been the look on my face that made the driver stop, because I didn't even raise my arms. He eased back on the reins and stood on the brake, and the coach slowed and finally jerked to a stop beside me.

"What on earth?" the driver asked.

"There are two dead men on the bank down-river," I said. "One is a murderer and the other was murdered. I am a witness and an intended victim, and I would be grateful for a ride to the authorities."

"Boy, howdy," the driver said. "I'd welcome you to Leadville, miss, but it seems you're already acquainted. Climb aboard. Make some room inside, gents. Just one of you get on top and shut up about it."

The door of the coach swung open.

"Obliged," I said.

Then I paused before pulling myself up.

"There's also a dead man, murdered, at Oro City."

"I'll take your word for it," the driver said. "Are

you all right? You're bleeding in a couple of places. Maybe you'd best see the old doc when you get into town."

"The marshal first," I said.

Taking my place among the eight men in the coach, I had plenty of elbow room. Nobody wanted to get too close to me.

Soon after reaching town a search party was organized and, before midnight, the bodies of Cade and the Sky Pilot were carried back to Leadville. The Lake County sheriff had already found the body of Hollister, and it, too, was taken to Leadville, where the coroner was kept busy all night. I was questioned for three hours by the sheriff and the city marshal, and then was examined by the coroner, who was also a town doctor. He said I might have a scar on my throat from the knife blade, and that Cade had loosened one of my teeth with his fist, but that my scratches and bruises would eventually heal and that, otherwise, I was fit enough.

A reporter for the Leadville paper, *Reveille*, asked to interview me, but I was too tired. I asked him to come back the next day.

I hadn't told the law officers about my notes from the library ledger, or the cipher that Hollister had given me, because I was afraid if they were entered into evidence, they would conveniently disappear. Afraid they would search me, I hid the paper in my underthings, but it was an unnecessary precaution. They went through the contents of the satchel, of course, and said they were going to keep the revolver as evidence in the murder of the preacher, and I had no objection because I had no use for guns. They also said they were going to search the river for the knife, but I knew they would never find it.

But I asked if I could keep the satchel.

A gruesome souvenir, I know, but I wanted it. At the very least, I had earned it.

I was allowed to leave with Augusta Tabor. She took me to the mercantile and after a bath and a light supper, I retired to the little sleeping room upstairs. Before I went to sleep, I picked up the hand mirror from the nightstand and gazed into it.

There was nothing there except my own bruised reflection.

32

At ten o'clock in the morning, I walked into The Great Divide in a fresh suit of clothes and with an eight-pound sledge that I had borrowed from Tabor Mercantile over my shoulder. The sledge had an octagonal, steel-forged head with a thirty-six-inch hickory handle. The only thing, I had decided that morning, was to be direct about my intentions.

"Hold on there," Francis Gallagher said, throwing his hands up. "You can't bring that thing in here."

"You told me to come back to see you, Frank. Here I am."

The bar was full of miners getting an early start in celebrating the Fourth of July, and they began to tease Gallagher about having his manhood flattened by an irate woman with a large hammer. The reporter from the *Reveille* had seen me walking down the street, obviously intent on mayhem, and he had fallen in behind me and was now standing to the side, furiously taking notes.

"You'd better move aside, Frank," I said.

I could see Horrible Hank floating in the mirror, his eyes wide.

"You're not intending to . . ."

"That's exactly my intent," I said. "Now, move aside so you don't get hurt."

Hank nodded wildly.

The miners hooted.

"Don't you want a drink first, Miss Wylde?" Gallagher said.

"No, Frank, I don't want a drink. Move the hell out of the way."

I was standing at the middle of the bar, one foot up on the brass rail, getting ready to heave the sledge at the mirror. Hank was trying to tell me something, but I couldn't hear him for all the commotion behind me.

"Can't hear you," I shouted.

Hank pointed to a spot three feet to the right of where I was standing.

"Right here," I heard him say.

I nodded.

"Let's talk this through," Gallagher pleaded. "Andrew Jackson Miles will have my head if I let anything happen to this mirror. That mirror is worth a fortune, and I can't let you do this."

"Andrew Jackson Miles is a horse thief and has commissioned murder and doesn't deserve a single vote for governor," I said. "Stand with him or stand aside."

Frank dove for cover as I drew back the sledge. "Duck, Hank!"

Now that the miners were sure I was going to do it, they rushed forward to stop me. But they were too late. Keeping my eyes fixed on the point Hank had indicated, I swung the sledge forward with both hands—and then let it fly.

It spun once in mid-air and then struck the mirror perfectly. The head sank into the quicksilvered glass as if it were water, and I turned away as the mirror exploded, shooting a geyser of glass shards spraying over the bar. The sound was like a thousand crystal tumblers shattering on a steel floor.

"Oh, no," Gallagher moaned.

I turned back.

Some cracked pieces of the mirror remained, mostly at the sides, and a few hung precariously from the top, like a mirror of Damocles, but where I had aimed there was nothing but a splintered backboard and a two-foot diameter hole that led into darkness. The sledge had passed completely through, and there wasn't even a sign of the yard-long hickory handle.

"Well done," Hank said, from the reflection in a shot glass on the bar.

Gallagher set off running.

"I bet he doesn't stop until he reaches Utah Territory," Hank said.

The miners came forward, their boots crunching on the glass, and they crawled over and around the bar to inspect the damage. They peered into the hole in the backboard, and then one of them said he felt cool air, and another called for a light. The miner took one of the candles offered, lit it, and thrust it through the hole.

"Do you see the sledge?" somebody asked.

"I see more than that," the miner said, and asked for help as he began to rip pieces of the backboard away, revealing the wall behind. The sledge had gone through the wall as well, and the miners began tearing at it, now using small hammers and pliers and whatever tools they had on them. Out came slats from packing crates, stamped with names like GIANT BLASTING POWDER and VIN MARIANA TONIC WINE. Then, when the hole was judged of sufficient size, more candles were lit and three of the thin miners squeezed through, one at a time.

"What is it?" somebody called. "Tell us."

A miner stuck his head through the hole.

"Miss, I think you want to see this," he said.

The miners helped me climb up to the hole, and being about as small as the smallest of the men, I was able to make my way through with only a little difficulty. I found myself standing in a drift, with aging timbers all around. The three miners were clustered to the side, their candles held low. One of them was in front, so I couldn't see.

"Move, dummy," one of the miners said, pulling him back.

A skeleton was slumped to the floor of the drift, chains crossing his shoulders. The skull was resting against the wall, and the jawbone had fallen to the bony chest, which was covered in a ragged plaid shirt. On the wall near him, but just out of reach, was a pickaxe.

"Who do you suppose he was?" one of the miners asked.

"Don't know, but he's been here a while. A long while."

"Miners always put their names on their tools," the third one said. He brushed the dust away from the handle of the pick with his hand, then brought the candle close and tilted his head to read the name.

But I already knew what he would say.

"Angus Wright."

We crawled back out of the hole in the broken mirror, and the last miner out handed me the eight-pound sledge I had borrowed.

"Thanks," I said. "I imagine Augusta Tabor will have this back, or know the reason why."

"What do we do with the . . . with the skeleton?" someone asked.

"Summon the marshal and the coroner," I said. "And then the undertaker can do his work. Angus Wright will finally get a proper burial, after all these years of waiting."

There were more questions from the miners, but I held up a hand.

"I'm tired, boys," I said. "And it's time for me to go home."

I stepped out onto the street and took a deep breath of the cool air.

The *Reveille* reporter stepped out with me, his hands in his pockets. He looked up at the cloud-flecked sky, then looked at me, and shook his head.

"How did you know what was behind the mirror?" he asked.

"I didn't," I said. "But I had my suspicions."

"Cade Harland, the murderer. He told you before he died."

"That was part of it."

"That makes sense," he said. "But tell me, who is Hank?"

I smiled.

"Son, there are some things a detective just doesn't reveal."

It began to snow then, big flakes drifting down to land in our hair and dust our shoulders. I reached out and caught a snowflake in the palm of my hand, where it quickly dissolved.

Then I set off walking, back to Tabor's Mercantile, to return the sledge and to gather my valise and other things, and to catch one of the twice-daily coaches for Denver.

33

The Denver Board of Education had put all of the crates from the recently closed library association in storage, in a warehouse on Blake Street, pending the construction of a new high school library. It took me the better part of one morning, and uncrating most of the 600 volumes that Patterson had boxed up, before I found *Syrinx of the Seven Worlds*.

It was then but a matter of minutes to decipher the coded message that Hollister had saved for all of those years (I was now carrying paper and pencil and other necessary things in the brown leather satchel, now my detection kit). The message was, indeed, instructions for Hollister and Miles to steal horses from an immigrant family camped near Auraria City.

After that, I visited Eureka Smith at his studio. After describing the events in Leadville, and what had been found behind the diamond dust mirror at The Great Divide, I had him photograph the old coded message, the relevant pages from *Syrinx*, and my copy of the library ledger list. Then I asked him to send copies to the biggest Denver papers and the Leadville *Reveille*.

The political career of Andrew Jackson Miles was over—already news of the discovery of the skeleton of Angus Wright had made it to Denver, and the Republican party made it clear that Frederick W. Pitkin would get the nomination—and be the next governor of Colorado.

But that wasn't enough, at least not for me. I wanted everyone to know the extent of his thieving and murderous deceit, and I wanted him prosecuted for it—although I knew convincing Decker or anyone else to bring charges based, in part, on spectral evidence was remote.

I asked Smith about his fraud charges, and he said the case had been withdrawn by Decker the day after my testimony. Then Smith asked me to have dinner with him, but I declined, saying I wasn't in the mood for fowl. But I did agree to have a cup of tea; then I asked to borrow twenty dollars, so I could buy a train ticket back to Dodge City.

He insisted I take forty.

As I left Smith's studio, two brutish men in derby hats and dark suits fell in beside me. They didn't speak, just crowded me so expertly that I was forced against a carriage at the curb side.

Fearing the worst, I turned and faced the pair.

"Hurt me," I said, "and you will surely regret it."

Behind me, the door of the landau opened.

"They're not going to hurt you, Miss Wylde," a voice called. "At least not until they are instructed to. Please, get in."

It was dark inside the carriage, because the shades were drawn, but I could see a man sitting inside, with his hands resting on top of a silver-knobbed cane.

"Councilman Miles," I said. "What an unpleasant surprise."

"Get in," Miles said, "or my men will toss you in."

"When you put it so nicely, how can I refuse?"

I stepped into the coach, taking the bench opposite Miles, and one of his thugs slammed the door after me. Then the driver cracked the whip and the landau jerked forward, then settled into a slow and steady rocking motion. Slowly, my eyes adjusted to the gloom inside.

"Where are we headed?"

"I assume you need a ride to the train station."

"I'd rather walk."

"Give me a few minutes of your time," Miles said. "After all, you have taken so much of mine."

He gave me a stare that was at once distant and menacing.

"I see you have a taken a prize," Miles said, indicating the brown leather satchel over my shoulder. "Do you hide a revolver in it as well?"

"It seemed appropriate to put it to less violent uses."

"It is odd to see someone other than Cade carry it," he said. "But then, change is the nature of life. One day you're on top of the world, and the next . . . well, the next you are waiting for indictments to be handed down."

"Eureka Smith says that you will serve no time."

"He may be right, but public pressure will demand that I be charged with something, and horse theft is still a capital crime," Miles said. "But it was so long ago and there are no witnesses save an obscure book and a scrap of paper. I assume both are in your newly acquired bag."

I didn't reply.

"You're safe," he said.

"Of course I am," I said. "I had photographs made."

"You would be safe enough anyway," he said. "If you stumbled now, I would be there to catch your fall, because anything bad that happens to you would just make it harder on me. It is hard enough already."

"I'd imagine it would be a relief to know that, in all probability, you aren't going to spend the rest of your life in prison."

"There are other punishments," Miles said. "The wreckage of a political career, for example. Having one's name dragged through the mud by the newspapers. The reduction of status in the eyes of one's family and friends. The loss of a certain beautiful cigar girl."

"Those aren't punishments," I said. "They are results of the choices you made, and they don't begin to reflect the pain and misery you've inflicted on others."

Miles smiled.

"Nobody's innocent," he said. "They would have done the same to me, if they'd had the chance. You, of all people, should know this. I have a complete dossier on your previous career as a confidence woman. What's the saying, you can't cheat an innocent man?"

"No, but you can kill one," I said.

Miles snorted.

"What, the insane preacher?"

"He was innocent."

But was he, I thought? Was he trying to drown me, or did he keep me under the water for so long because he was afraid Cade would shoot me, too? I had turned it over in my mind a thousand times and had yet to reach a conclusion. And I knew I never would.

"I have a proposition, Miss Wylde."

"I've seen your work. Not interested."

"The damage could be contained," he said softly. "There is only your word for what Cade Harland and Ben Hollister said about my involvement, and you haven't given details to the press, or been asked under oath, at least not yet. I can't deny that I was involved in some youthful indiscretion—my word, who wasn't?—but it is possible, with your help, to shape this in such a way as to mitigate my involvement. A. C. Ford was the real mastermind, and then Hollister took over after his death, and Cade was the homicidal maniac who began tracking down . . . Well, you see what I mean."

"You still wouldn't be governor."

"No, not anytime soon," he said. "But the public has a very short memory. Allow a few years to pass, create a home for orphans, build a library or two, endow a university here in Denver. Become the Leland Stanford of the Rocky Mountains."

I didn't reply.

"You would be richly compensated, of course."

"Of course," I said.

I took the Brothers Upmann from my breast pocket—the cigar I had paid too much for in exchange for information—and removed the wrapper. It had been only slightly bent during the course of the adventure.

"You cannot imagine the kind of wealth I speak of," Miles said. "What is the most you've ever held in your hand at one time, even during the best years of your trance medium days? Five hundred dollars?"

"I was much better than that."

"A thousand dollars? Imagine a thousand dollars as pin money."

He produced a small knife, took the cigar, and notched the end for me.

"You could leave Kansas forgotten and far behind," he said, producing a match and lighting the cigar. "You could return to a city where you feel more at home—Chicago, or St. Louis, or New York. Think of the art, of the culture, of the ease of life."

I sucked flame into the cigar.

"Ah, yes," he said. "I can see the thought excites you."

I puffed and was surprised by the taste—a combination of oak leaves and coffee, if that mix were smoldering and about to spontaneously combust. There was also an acrid aftertaste that trickled down my throat, and I fought the urge to gag.

The landau pulled over and stopped. We had arrived at the station.

"What excites me," I said, exhaling smoke, "is the thought of you, a broken and pathetic man, living out the rest of your days in that monument to incomplete dreams and unfulfilled ambition you call a saloon at Leadville. I knew the moment I saw the saloon that it was a manifestation of your authentic personality, a clue to your loathsome and self-defeating nature. I am not interested in your money, Councilman Miles. And before too long, you won't have any money to offer anybody to do your killing and lying for you, because it will have all been taken by those who are like you, but stronger, and who don't have to answer to the charge of horse thief, no matter whether you serve time or not."

I stepped out of the carriage, took a last drag on the cigar, and threw it into the gutter.

"Thanks for the ride," I said.

* * *

I hadn't slept well for a fortnight, and had slept barely at all in the last seventy-two hours. Every time I drifted off to sleep, I found myself on the dream train, on the way to Brookwood Cemetery. It was no different on the trip back home. It was late in the afternoon when the Denver & Rio Grande train pulled out of the station on its way to Pueblo. After a short wait, and a dinner of toast and coffee, I boarded the Santa Fe eastbound, and began the long and gradual descent to the plains of Kansas.

For most of the night, I stared out the coach window at the dark prairie rushing by. Periodically, Hank would appear in the glass, but sensing my mood and perhaps chastened by his brief entrapment in the diamond dust mirror, he left me mostly to my thoughts.

I was afraid to sleep, for fear the next dream aboard the death train might tip me over into insanity—or that I would impulsively decide to get off the train at Brookwood Cemetery when it arrived, just to have things done with.

But perhaps none of it was real anyway.

Perhaps I had been mad all along.

It was 102 degrees when I walked with my valise up the steps to the Dodge House and paid the twenty-three dollars I owed in back rent. At least, that's what Jimmy said the official weather station on top of the hotel had recorded just minutes before.

"They say it might get as high as a hundred and ten in August," he said.

"Something to look forward to," I said.

"Are you coming back to the hotel?" Jimmy asked. "Your room is still open."

Paying the hotel had wiped me out, once again. Between it and the train ticket, I had one dollar and twenty-seven cents left.

"I don't know, Jimmy. We'll have to see."

Determined to run up no more debt, I picked up the valise and walked out the door. It was another Sunday and hardly a soul was moving on Front Street. I was tired and longed to put my feet up and simply rest, but there was a stop I had to make first.

It took me only a few minutes to walk to the house on Chestnut Street with the two pear trees out front. I knocked on the door, and in a few moments Molly Howart appeared.

"Miss Wylde," she said. "Do come in."

Molly Howart was wearing a dark bombazine dress trimmed in black crepe. She invited me into the room where Charlie Howart had been found hanging. It was the same, with the exception that the windows were open and the curtains drawn, and a bit of black cloth hung over each.

"Would you care for some tea?" she asked.

"No, thank you," I said. Etiquette may have required I take the tea, but what I really wanted was a strong cup of coffee, but I could not bring myself to trouble the widow. We sat in the straight-backed chairs and Molly held her restless hands in her lap and waited for me to begin.

"Charlie did not commit suicide," I said.

Tears of relief welled in her eyes.

"How do you know?"

"His killer told me before he, himself, was slain," I said. "His name was Cade Harland, and he came here to silence Charlie and to recover the book he possessed, but accomplished only one of his goals. Had he found the book, the crime would have gone unsolved, because our only clue would have been the train ticket to Canon City, and that would have been a dead end."

"But why did Charlie have that ticket?" she asked. "Was he planning on . . . ?"

"No, he did not intend to abandon you," I said. "His intent, I believe, was to travel to Leadville and uncover evidence that would have exposed Andrew Jackson Miles and provided some safety for the both of you. But there are two ways to get to Leadville, and each take about the same time from Dodge City. One goes via Pueblo and Denver, as I went, and the other goes to the end of the tracks at Canon City. From there, a stage line provides service up the Arkansas River valley. He choose the Canon City route, I think, to avoid Denver—and Jackson Davis Miles and his thugs."

She nodded.

"What about the life insurance policy?"

"Once I describe what I've learned to our coroner, Doc McCarty, the official finding will be changed to murder," I said. "Mister Clement Hill of the Western Mutual Life Assurance Company will then be forced to approve your claim, all five thousand dollars of it."

Molly Howart leaned forward and squeezed my hand.

As I walked from Molly Howart's home toward the agency, I thought about Molly Howart's security in the form of the $5,000 policy—and I thought about my own lack of means. I couldn't even bring myself to ask for my wages from her, at least not until she received her due from the insurance company. As I passed Beatty and Kelly's Restaurant, I considering stopping for a large cup of coffee, with real cream, but didn't; I had to make the dollar and twenty-seven cents in my pocket go as far as possible.

I pressed on.

Suddenly the doors to the Alamo Saloon burst open and Hickory Lane staggered out, tossing a string of obscenities at those inside.

"Think a you're too good for me?" she howled. "Let a me tell you, I've been a kicked out of fancier places than a this. Some a day, you'll be a beggin' me to come a back."

She took a few unsteady steps into the street, then turned and saw me walking toward her. She had obviously been on an all-night and most-of-the-day bender.

"Look a here," Hickory said. "Curious cat a walkin' like she the Queen of England. Well, I a think she need the curious beat a right out of her."

I said nothing. I was too tired for it.

"Didn't you a hear?" Hickory asked, stepping in front of me.

I stopped.

"I heard, Hickory," I said. "You want to beat me up."

"Don't that a scare you?"

"No, Hickory, it doesn't," I said. "At least you're honest in your dislike of me. That's good, because I can deal with that, I can plan around it. It's the people who smile and pretend they're your friends and then break your heart—those are the ones who scare me."

Then I walked around her.

When I unlocked the door to the agency, Eddie greeted me.

"Weak and weary!"

"Quite," I said.

Eddie ruffled his feathers and gave a terrible screech, to show his displeasure at my having left him for so long. A week must seem like a month to him.

"I'm sorry," I cooed. "Next time, I'll take you with me."

Doc McCarty had taken good care of him, because there was plenty of food and water in his cage. McCarty had also placed a railway express letter on my desk, one that he had accepted in my absence. While Eddie chattered behind me, I looked at the return address.

It was from Old Statehouse Publishing Co. in Boston.

Dear Miss Wylde,

 Thank you for your kind letter.

 I am sorry to inform you that Capt. William L. Gresham, author of Syrinx of the Seven Worlds *and other metaphysical volumes published by our house, escaped this mortal coil a few days before we received your inquiry. He succumbed to pneumonia and lingering complications from spiritual wounds sustained during the late war. Your queries regarding his novel must, of necessity, remain unanswered at present.*

 He had attained the biblical measure of three score and ten years.

 Capt. Gresham was a fervent Abolitionist, a leading Spiritualist, and a courageous supporter of Women's Suffrage. He was a native New Englander, and the last living descendant of Revolutionary War hero Major Leland Gresham. A confirmed bachelor, Capt. Gresham left no survivors and asked that what remained of a once-considerable family fortune be given to the Charity for the Houseless Poor, at Lowell, Mass.

 Because of your interest in Capt. Gresham's work, I have taken the liberty of enclosing a subscription card for his forthcoming book, a

*posthumous account of his service during the
Civil War. It is entitled,* An Occult History of
the LaDue Survival Brigade. *This is a most
anticipated book, because of the brigade's
valiant but ultimately tragic efforts in the
Bloody Trench during the Battle of
Spottsylvania Courthouse in 1864.*

*Capt. Gresham was, as you may be aware, an
eyewitness to the brigade's final hours, and we
are fortunate that he left us his testament before
being called away.*

*Obediently yours,
Garrick Sloane, publisher*

I felt the floor turn topsy-turvy and had to grasp
the desk to keep from falling. Could Gresham
have known anything about how Jonathan died?
Would he have put the details in the book? Not
knowing the details of his death had gnawed at
me, always. Even though I had given up the
séances in which I had tried without success for
years to contact Jonathan on the other side, I still
longed for a piece of solid information about his
end. I especially wanted to know his last words and,
selfishly and eternally, if he had mentioned me.

I determined to borrow three dollars from Doc
McCarty to order the book and find out. So much
for staying out of debt.

The bell above the door of the agency jangled
as Jack Calder walked in.

He had a rifle slung over his shoulder, held a
fistful of papers, and was caked in trail dust. He

walked over to his desk, threw the papers down, leaned the rifle against the wall, and sat wearily in the chair.

"Tough day?" I asked.

"Tough two weeks," he said. "Harker was easy, but Smilin' Solomon Stone made a run for it. Had to chase him all the way to Bell County, Texas, and damn near had to kill him before I could get him in irons. But he's in the Ford County Jail now."

"So you didn't lose the bond."

"Not this time," he said. "What have you been up to?"

"Something I could have used your help on. Especially your two-fisted, upper body strength kind of help."

"Yeah?" he said. "That what happened to your face?"

"Yes."

"You all right?"

"Yes."

"How'd it happen?"

"I was on a case," I said. "It began—"

Calder held up his hand.

"I'm sorry, Ophie," he said. "You're okay, and that's the important thing. But I'm beat and have to get some rest. I'm dead tired. I'd love to hear about it, but tomorrow."

"All right," I said. "But tomorrow, Jack, we really have to talk."

He nodded.

"I'm going home," he said.

He started for the door, then stopped.

"Oh, I found something in my vest that I think is yours," he said, pulling a railway ticket from his vest. "Don't know how it got there. Had a weird dream of us being on a train, but it didn't make any sense. Did you go to Iowa at some point without me knowing about it?"

"Iowa?" I asked.

"Yeah, it says Waterloo on it."

I snatched the ticket from his hand.

"Oh, Jack!"

It was the temporary pass, Number 000.

I threw my arms around him. Then I backed away.

"Oh, Jack," I said. "You need a bath."

"It had crossed my mind."

"And just because I hugged you," I said, "doesn't mean we don't have to talk tomorrow, so plan on it. If we're going to be partners, we've got to work together—and you have to stop being mad at me for handling the spook end of it and not being able to charge clients."

"On this case of yours," he said. "Did you make any—"

"I mean it, Jack."

"Yeah, I got it," he said. "Tomorrow."

He shut the door behind him.

I clutched the ticket tightly. Then I started arranging a little sleeping space in the back of the office, using the blankets and other things I'd brought from the Dodge House when I'd moved out. It wouldn't be as comfortable as my old bed in Room 217, but I was so tired I didn't care.

34

The train is stopped. On one side, there is a depot that looks more like a chapel than a railway station, and on the other, a vast park with gentle green hills that seem to roll on forever.

The other passengers have already exited the train. Some are still on the platform, talking, while others are strolling arm in arm across the grounds. Only the old man and I are left in the car.

The white-glove conductor walks down the aisle toward us.

"Brookwood," he says gently. "Time to get off, Captain Gresham."

"What?"

"We've arrived. It's time."

The old man nods, resigned.

"You're W. L. Gresham?" I ask.

"I was."

"Captain William L. Gresham? The author of Syrinx of the Seven Worlds?"

"Why, yes."

For the first time, he smiles.

"You're familiar with it?"

"Intimately," I say. "And I'm looking forward to your new book."

He grasps my hand.

"It is time, sir," the conductor says.

"You don't know how happy you've made me," Gresham says.

"What about you, miss?" the conductor asks. "Getting off here?"

"No," I say. "I have found the temporary pass."

"You have indeed," he says. "Take that right back to the superintendent and he'll fix you up. And, if you'll allow me to say so, I'm right proud of you. Not just for the ticket—for all of it."

He takes Gresham's elbow and leads him to the door.

"But wait," I say. "I have to ask about the brigade."

"No time, miss," the conductor says. "Superintendent's waiting."

Gresham turns and waves.

I sigh.

"Guess I'll just have to read the book," I tell myself.

I walk toward the back of the train, through the empty coffin car, where the widdershins are lolling about and playing pinochle and eating the most awful-smelling snacks. I hold my breath and hurry to the private car at the end of the train.

"You found the pass," Death says. "Congratulations and all that. Now hand it over."

He snaps his fingers.

"So rude!"

"Schedules to keep," he says, taking the pass from me.

He opens a drawer and drops it in, then picks up a pen and scribbles a note in the ledger.

"Speaking of schedules," I say. "Tell me when I'm going to die."

"Against policy."

"None of this has been exactly according to policy, has it?" I ask. "Tell me."

He puts the pen down.

"You don't really want to know," he says.

"Yes, I do."

"Well, I won't tell you," he says. "People aren't meant to know if they'll outlive their children, or their friends, or even their pets. Do you want to know when Eddie is going to die? Of course not. It would be cruel. You could never enjoy another day together without thinking of that awful date."

"But the awful date comes, whether we think of it or not."

Death drums his fingers.

"The reason for the policy is this," he says. "If a person knew with absolute confidence when they were going to die, years or even decades in advance, then it would be a kind of temporary immortality, as oxymoronic as that sounds. One could engage in any kind of behavior without fear of a fatal outcome. For the human of average sensibility, this might mean the taking of outlandish risks for amusement. For the subaverage, it could mean stunts that would encourage belief in miracles, the founding of religions, or fostering an unstoppable dictatorship that would enslave humanity until the fateful day."

"*And how would this differ from what we have now, exactly?*"

Death sighs.

"*This much I will tell you,*" he says. "*You will move to London. You will have incredible joy and unbearable heartbreak. You will witness the passing of one age and the beginning of the next. Your life will be, at turns, mundane and remarkable—as all lives are. And you will be buried here, at Brookwood Cemetery. That's as specific as I can be.*"

"*At least it's something,*" I say.

"*Do try to keep from crossing wires with us in the future.*"

"*This last case turned out all right, didn't it?*"

"*If you mean you came close to having yourself drowned, driven mad, and murdered, then yes,*" he says. "*Personally, I can't see the fun in any of it. That business with the book and the numbers—so elementary! But the spirit photo, that was a bit interesting.*"

"*How did you know about it?*"

"*Our branch was involved in picking up a number of passengers associated with your adventure, and I don't mind telling you the widdershins had a devil of a time keeping you from spotting them, seeing as you had one foot on the platform and the other on the train, as it were.*"

Death pauses.

"*A word of advice, Miss Wylde,*" he says. "*Captain Gresham's publisher will be looking for new authors, and you have been working for some time to scribble out your first adventure—what is it?—the* Mystery of the

Girl Betrayed. *You might submit to them. Writing books could be a way of making a living at helping people, in your own fashion, without cadging nickels and dimes."*

Of course. Why hadn't I thought of that?

"Until we meet again, in another five or fifty years—adieu!"